John George Brighton

Admiral of the Fleet, Sir Provo W. P. Wallis, G.C.B.

A Memoir

John George Brighton

Admiral of the Fleet, Sir Provo W. P. Wallis, G.C.B.
A Memoir

ISBN/EAN: 9783337103750

Printed in Europe, USA, Canada, Australia, Japan

Cover: Foto ©Raphael Reischuk / pixelio.de

More available books at **www.hansebooks.com**

ADMIRAL OF THE FLEET

SIR PROVO W. P. WALLIS,

G.C.B., Etc.

A Memoir

BY

J. G. BRIGHTON, M.D.,

AUTHOR OF "A MEMOIR OF ADMIRAL SIR P. B. V. BROKE, BART.," ETC.

WITH NUMEROUS ILLUSTRATIONS, CHARTS, ETC.

LONDON:

HUTCHINSON & CO.,

25, PATERNOSTER SQUARE,

1892.

TO

HER MOST GRACIOUS MAJESTY

THE QUEEN

THIS MEMOIR OF

ADMIRAL OF THE FLEET

SIR PROVO WALLIS, G.C.B.,

IS DEDICATED

BY HER MAJESTY'S

SPECIAL GRACIOUS PERMISSION.

PREFACE.

ABOUT the year 1854, being detained at Salisbury waiting for the train, I strolled into a book shop and purchased a volume published in the United States relating the events of the war between those States and Great Britain in 1812, 1813, 1814, and 1815. I read it carefully, with amazement at my own ignorance. I had scarcely heard of any such war! And why? Because in those years we had a war, and a tremendous one it was, with almost all the European powers, at our own doors.

"Here, Boney, come and take this naughty little boy!" was the common style used to cow unruly lads; and "Sarah, look to my sword, pistol, and spurs; we are called out," to the wife; and to the servant, "William, feed my charger, saddle and bring him round." So ordered the cavalry yeoman, almost daily, down to 1815.

No wonder little or nothing was heard of the war raging in America and Canada, 3000 miles distant. Consequently I had, so to speak, to put myself to school again. I read all the books I could find on the subject, visited America, made the acquaintance of various actors in the now far past; and, as far as possible, put myself in possession of all authentic records concerning the struggle which had taken place.

Among the many who cheerfully responded to my inquiries, were—1st, the ever-to-be-lamented Admiral Sir George Broke-Middleton, sole surviving son of the captain of the *Shannon*. I have spoken elsewhere (in the Memoir of his father) of all his kind and valuable assistance. 2ndly, the revered subject of this Memoir, Admiral of the Fleet Sir Provo W. P. Wallis—now in his 101st year, and undeniably the sole survivor of that, the last conflict, I trust, with our brethren across the Atlantic.

I little thought, when we exchanged our first letters in 1863, that it was the beginning of a lifelong correspondence and most affectionate friendship. But here is his first letter :—

" FUNTINGTON, CHICHESTER, *Jan. 1st*, 1864.
" REV. SIR,—
  " If you will call at the United Service Club, Pall Mall, on Thursday, the 7th inst. (from twelve to two o'clock), you will find me (D.V.) there, in readiness to receive you. Pray excuse a short reply, being anxious to save to-day's post; but believe me, rev. Sir,

    " Yours very faithfully, PROVO WALLIS."

Of course I duly kept this appointment, and found myself in the presence of the Admiral.

He was then seventy-three years of age, but did not look sixty.

I stated my object in few words, and in reply received the pleasant answer: "Any information in my power, sir, I shall feel most happy to supply."

I had prepared a short paper to this effect, which we patiently debated. In about an hour, reluctant to intrude further, I rose to retire.

"May I ask if you are staying at the Victoria?" he inquired.

"I have been, but shall leave to-night by the Irish mail, after dinner." And so we parted; but at four o'clock, just as the cold, raw, snowy, windy afternoon was closing, I was surprised by a most unexpected return visit from the Admiral, who had walked some four miles to see me. We had a long and interesting conversation, ended by him, as he rose to go, with the words, "I hope you will write to me whenever you feel disposed." My readers will see, in the following pages, that I did not fail to do so.

CONTENTS.

CHAPTER I.

BIRTH, PARENTAGE, AND EARLY DAYS.

CHAPTER II.

THE *SHANNON* AND SOME OF HER EXPLOITS.

CHAPTER III.

NOVA SCOTIA—FURTHER EXPLOITS OF THE *SHANNON*.

CHAPTER IV.

THE BLOCKADE OF BOSTON, AND CAPTURE OF THE U.S. FRIGATE *CHESAPEAKE*.

CHAPTER V.

THE VOYAGE TO HALIFAX AND RECEPTION THERE.

CHAPTER VI.

AT HALIFAX.

CHAPTER VII.

CHAPTER VIII.

WALLIS'S FURTHER SERVICES AND APPOINTMENTS.

CHAPTER IX.

LIST OF ILLUSTRATIONS.

I.

BIRTH, PARENTAGE, AND EARLY DAYS.

CHAPTER I.

" Oh yes, smile for smile, heart for heart, kindness for kindness, welcome
    for welcome—give me old Nova Scotia yet—there ain't nothin' like it
    here."—*Sam Slick.*

IN the year 1791 Halifax, in the Colony of
Nova Scotia, presented rather a primitive
appearance, notwithstanding it was, and for years
had been, the great and popular military and naval
rendezvous of British North America. The town
itself mainly consisted of wooden houses. There
were, however, public buildings of greater pretension,
more solidly constructed—the Government House,
the Fort, and the residences of the officials in His
Majesty's Navy Yard.

Among the latter was that of Provo Featherstone
Wallis, Esq., Chief Clerk to the Commissioner of the
Yard.

Here, on April 12th, in the above-mentioned year,
was born his only son, Provo William Parry, who

afterwards became Sir Provo W. P. Wallis, G.C.B.,
Senior Admiral of the British Fleet.

Our hero's mother was a daughter of William
Lawlor, Major in the 1st Battalion of the Halifax
(Nova Scotia) Regiment, and it has been suggested
that his father was intimately connected with Captain
Samuel Wallis, who commanded the *Dolphin* on her
celebrated voyage round the Globe, 1766 to 1768,
and discovered several important islands which were
added to England's domains, and after whom Wallis
Island, the Wallis Islets, the Wallis Mark Rock, and
the Wallis Shoal were named, and also with Gilbert
Wallis, who died while in command of the *Port Mahon*
in 1740, but there appear to be no authentic records
to prove that this belief is well founded.   Whether it
be so or not, it is clear that our hero's father was an
admirer of the naval profession, and that he chose it
for his son almost as soon as he was born.

It may be interesting to some to note, bearing in
mind that two of Sir Provo's Christian names are
William and Parry, that his birth took place in the
year immediately following that in which the renowned Arctic explorer, Captain William Edward
Parry, was born ; and that in 1813, at the time of the
famous action between the *Shannon* and *Chesapeake*,
in which Wallis took such an active part, they were
both occupied on the North American Station—Wallis
in the *Shannon* and Parry in *La Hogue*—Parry at
this time visiting Wallis's birthplace.

In one of the letters written to me by the Admiral after he was well advanced in years, he says that he was at an early age sent to England for his education; but this appears to be the only available record of his childhood beyond the two or three facts we will now mention.

At the time of his birth a custom prevailed which enabled influential relatives or friends to get a boy's name entered on a ship's books as one of her crew, notwithstanding he did not actually join her, and was, indeed, too young to do so. It was, in fact, a time when, as Mr. Laird Clowes has quaintly said, "There were bishops in bibs, and colonels in short frocks." Competitive examinations were almost, if not quite, unknown, and influence rather than merit was paramount. It thus happened that, through the influence of his father or the friends of the latter, young Wallis, on May 1st, 1795, and when but four years of age, was entered on the books of the *Oiseau* frigate, which was employed on the Halifax Station, as one of her *able-bodied* seamen. Able-bodied as he probably was for his years, it is hardly necessary to say he did not then actually go to sea, at least, to perform those duties which properly belonged to the position in which he had been placed.

From May 1796 until September 1798 he served nominally in the *Prévoyante* as a first-class volunteer, and from May 1799 until September 1800 did imaginary service in the *Asia* with Captain Robert Murray, who had previously commanded the *Oiseau*, when Wallis was fictitiously with her. He subsequently joined the *Cleopatra*, a smart 12-pounder 32-gun frigate, Captain Israel Pellew (afterwards Admiral Sir Israel Pellew), and did nominal service in her as a midshipman, and later, viz., in October 1804, he, as a midshipman, actually joined that ship, which was then under the command of Captain Sir Robert Laurie, and actively commenced his career at a time when our country was in open hostility with France. Even then he was but little more than thirteen years old— young enough, one would say, to begin active service; yet the great Nelson, who was then living and who had still to win Trafalgar, began earlier, by going to sea at the age of twelve.

From this time all Wallis's services were real, and being a fine, manly lad he, doubtless, entered upon them eagerly and with pleasure.

It is curious that O'Byrne, in his "Naval Dictionary," should treat all Wallis's early services seriously. Sir Provo himself says: "All that O'Byrne states in reference to my services previously to 1804 is only moonshine. My real career commenced from the time I joined the *Cleopatra*, in October 1804."

The *Cleopatra* soon sailed for the North American Station, and Wallis had not been with her many months before he saw what active service meant, for on February 17th, 1805, he was present at his first engagement, and a desperate one it proved.

It will be my object, whenever possible, to use the words of those present at the events to be related. The following account of the engagement just referred to was written by Admiral Wallis himself, years after the action :—

"We sailed for the North American Station, and on the 16th of February, 1805, at daylight (lat. 20° N., long. 67° W.), came in sight of a ship standing to the eastward. All sail was made in chase; but it was not until ten in the morning of the 17th that she was overtaken. The stranger was the French 18-pounder 40-gun frigate *Ville de Milan*. At 11.30 a.m. the latter, having shortened sail and hauled to the wind, hoisted her colours; and the *Cleopatra*, having also shortened sail, fired her bow guns and commenced a running fight.

"At 2.30 p.m., the *Cleopatra* being within a hundred yards of her antagonist, the *Ville de Milan* luffed across the bows of the British ship, and opened her broadside. The *Cleopatra*, passing under her adversary's stern, returned the fire, and, ranging up within musket-shot on the starboard side of the enemy, a determined fight took place, both ships running parallel to each other, sometimes nearly before the wind and at others close-hauled.

"At 5 p.m., having shot away the main-topsail-yard of the *Ville de Milan*, the *Cleopatra* forged ahead, and her running rigging being so much cut that she could neither shorten sail nor back her main-topsail, her captain determined to endeavour to cross the bows of the enemy. Just as the *Cleopatra* was putting her helm down for this purpose, a shot disabled her wheel. The French frigate, observing the ungovernable state of her antagonist, bore up, and ran her on board, the bowsprit and figure-head passing over the quarter-deck abaft the main rigging. From the commanding position of her adversary, owing to the strong wind and heavy sea running, the *Cleopatra* was in danger of being sunk by her heavy opponent. The French crew, in their attempts to board, were at first repulsed with loss; but about 5.15 p.m. the overpowering numbers of the assailants overcame all opposition, and the British colours were hauled down. Shortly afterwards the *Cleopatra's* fore and main masts went over the side, and the bowsprit soon followed.

"In this desperate action the *Cleopatra* had only 200 men at quarters, and of this number 16 seamen, 3 marines, and 1 boy were killed; there being a total of 22 mortally wounded or killed, and 36 wounded. Captain Renaud, of the *Ville de Milan*, was killed by the last shot fired from the *Cleopatra*; and her loss, although not stated, was also heavy.

"The *Ville de Milan* was a ship of 1100 tons, mounted 46 heavy guns—long 18- and 8-pounders— and had on board 350 men; whereas the *Cleopatra* carried 690 tons only, and was armed with long 12-pounders and 24-pounder carronades.

" Having removed the prisoners and put on board 49 officers and men, the prize and *Ville de Milan* (whose main and mizen masts having fallen during the night, was consequently also jury-rigged) continued their course homeward ; but on the 23rd of February Nemesis was in waiting, and they descried the 50-gun ship *Leander* (Captain the Hon. John Talbot), which ship immediately chased.

" The weather coming on thick the *Leander* lost sight of the frigates, but at 2.30 p.m. again obtained a view of them. The *Ville de Milan* and *Cleopatra* closed for mutual support, and having fired a gun to leeward, each hoisted a French ensign upon the mainstay. At 4 o'clock the *Leander* arrived within gunshot and the frigates separated, the *Cleopatra* running before the wind, and the *Ville de Milan* hauling up with the wind on the larboard quarter. At 4.30 the *Leander* fired a shot at the *Cleopatra,* upon which the French colours were hauled down and the ship hove to. Those of the original crew of the *Cleopatra* who remained on board then rushed upon deck and took possession of the ship, and Captain Talbot, directing the *Cleopatra* to follow, immediately pursued the *Ville de Milan.* Before 6 p.m., the *Leander* having got alongside the *Ville de Milan,* that ship surrendered without firing a shot. The French ship was added to the British Navy under the name of the *Milan,* and classed as an 18-pounder 38-gun frigate.'

It will thus be seen that our young midshipman, then less than fourteen years of age, was for a week or so a prisoner under the tricolour for the first and, as it happened, the last time. It was not, however, destined that this should be the only desperate action in which he was to share.

Wallis escaped injury during the engagement, and was, with the other prisoners, treated most kindly by the victors.

After the action Captain Talbot placed Sir R. Laurie again in command of the *Cleopatra*, and gave his own first lieutenant charge of the *Ville de Milan*, and all arrived safely in a British port.

This action was indeed a " seasoning " for our young midshipman. More than seventy years afterwards the terrible surroundings were vividly present to his memory—the roar of the artillery, the oaths of the combatants, the groans of the wounded, the decks streaming with blood, and, finally, the rush of the hostile boarders with fierce execrations—these indeed were enough to appal the nerves of the bravest ; but they did not damp the naval ardour glowing in our young hero's breast, nor diminish his love for his chosen profession. He returned with alacrity to his midshipman's duty, until some little time afterwards he was transferred to the *Cambrian*, 48, in the West Indies. It was in this ship he was serving when the thrilling news of Trafalgar and the glorious death of Nelson reached the *Cambrian's* crew. From this time onward, until 1812, we have not much more than a summary of his professional life ; and after making a record of some of its salient points, I propose devoting a few pages to a description of that cradle of renowned men, Nova Scotia, and that most dangerous station for susceptible young military and naval officers, Halifax—but this can wait.

My readers will be pleased to understand that this memoir is more of an autobiography than perhaps the generality of lives of eminent men—I mean, that it will, as far as possible, be framed on the venerable admiral's own letters, such notes and comments being added as that text and the lapse of time seem to require.

The captured frigate *Ville de Milan* having been added to the British navy and re-named the *Milan*, the command was given to Sir Robert Laurie, and Wallis continued to serve with him in that vessel on the coast of North America until his nomination as acting-lieutenant of the *Triumph*, 74, which took place on November 6th, 1806. The commander of this ship was Sir Thomas Masterman Hardy, that much-loved friend of Nelson, who was with him in his dying hours, and who has been more familiarly called "Nelson's Hardy." In February 1808 Wallis was placed as master's mate on board the *Bellona*, 74, Captain John Erskine Douglas, and on November 30th following was made a lieutenant and appointed to the 16-gun brig, *Curieux*. This vessel was commanded first by Captain Andrew Hodge, and subsequently by the Hon. George Moysey. Under the command of the latter the *Curieux* was engaged in the blockade of Guadaloupe, and succeeded in cutting out a privateer from St. Anne's Bay, but was soon afterwards wrecked upon the island of Petit Tene. Wallis, however, escaped from this peril, as all hands were fortunately saved. The vessel, he says, was afterwards burnt.

On November 29th, 1809, a few weeks after the wreck of the *Curieux*, Wallis was appointed lieutenant of the *Gloire*, a 38-gun frigate, which, like the *Curieux*, had been taken from the French. She was commanded by Captain James Carthew, and while in her Wallis assisted in the destruction, on December 18th, 1809, of two French 44-gun frigates, the *Loire* and the *Seine*, and also in the capture of the French batteries at Anse-la-Barque, which protected them, previously to the surrender of the island of Guadaloupe. For his services in these actions, and in respect of the capture of the island, at which Wallis was also present, he received a medal, which was not, however, granted until many years later.

In 1810 Wallis was transferred to the *Observateur*, Captain Frederick Augustus Wetherall; thence to the *Driver*, first serving in this ship under Captain John Lawrence, and later under Captain Thomas Swinnerton Dyer; and, on the *Driver* being paid off, was appointed to the *Emulous*, Captain William Howe Mulcaster.

II.

THE "SHANNON"—SOME OF HER EXPLOITS.

CHAPTER II.

WALLIS'S next ship was one which was destined to soon become famous. The *Shannon*, a fine 38-gun frigate, had been cruising under the command of Captain Philip Bowes Vere Broke for several years, without seeing much of the enemy, when Wallis was appointed one of her lieutenants. He joined this ship in January 1812, at Bermuda, respecting the state of which at that time it may not be out of place to say a few words.

The Bermudese islands are not often visited now; their palmy days of the war time, when the fast-sailing schooners, built of native cedar and pine, mocked an enemy's pursuit, are for ever gone. In 1812 they were of greater consequence, as the following list of government officials will show :—

Bermuda.

Governor, Sir James Cockburn, Bart.
President of Council, Hon. S. Trotter.
Secretary and Provincial Master General, Hon. R. Kennedy.
Treasurer, W. Smith, Esq.
Judge Admiralty Court, W. Territ, Esq.
Chief Justice, J. C. Esten, Esq.
King's Advocate, J. Christie, Esq.
Attorney-General, F. Forbes, Esq.
Registrar, T. Moore, Esq.
Collector, J. Stewart, Esq.
Surveyor, J. Tucker, Esq.

These islands were discovered by John Bermudas, a Spaniard, in 1527. They were nearly four hundred in number, but very few of them habitable. The principal was St. George's, sixteen miles long and three in breadth. There were but two places on this island where a ship could safely come near the shore, and these were covered with such high rocks that they required a pilot. St. George's Town was the principal haven, and was defended by nine forts and seventy cannon. Here it was that Wallis was introduced to his gallant shipmates of the *Shannon*, whom I must now make known to the reader.

Captain Broke was then thirty-seven years of age. Judging from his portrait by Lane (who by the way was deaf and dumb, but a favourite pupil of Lawrence), taken after Broke had become renowned in history, he was a fine, manly-looking officer. His hair was red, and undisguised by powder and the pigtail then going out of fashion ; his features frank

CAPTAIN BROKE, *Page 17.*

COMMANDER OF H.M.S. "SHANNON."

and open, his form symmetrical, his manner most
courteous, and in command and on duty most decisive.   At his table and in society he was most
winning and agreeable.   In his domestic relations
he could not be excelled.   Little wonder is it that
his officers and crew were ready to second such a
leader to the last.   He died an admiral in 1841,
aged sixty-five years.

The *Shannon's* first lieutenant, Watt, was more
than six feet in height, was strongly built, and was
as brave as he was big.   After fighting with the
greatest courage in the famous action we shall shortly
describe, he was numbered among the slain, through
a grape-shot inadvertently fired by his own friends
on to the decks of the enemy's ship, which he had
boarded.

The third lieutenant, Charles Leslie Falkiner, was
also (as one of his brother-officers described him)
"as fine a fellow as ever lived, and a capital messmate."   At the time of the *Shannon's* action with the
Chesapeake he was only twenty-four years of age.
After his ship was paid off he went afloat no more,
but, succeeding to the family baronetcy, died Sir
Charles Falkiner, 1858, aged sixty-nine years.

Wallis was second lieutenant, and, as his portrait
at the age of twenty-two indicates, was a strikingly
handsome young man.   He was also tall and well-
proportioned, brave, amiable, and good-tempered.
Little, no doubt, did he anticipate the lofty rank and

2

great age Providence had in store for him in years to come.

The other officers of the *Shannon* were these :—

Master, I. Burns; surgeon, A. Jack; purser, G. Aldham; gunner, R. Meehan; boatswain, Stevens; midshipmen, Smith, Etough, King, Clavering, Leake, Samwell, Fenn (captain's aide-de-camp), and Stevenson (absent as prize master). Marine officers: first, Lieutenant. Johns; second, Lieutenant Law. The crew numbered 306.

The *Shannon* sailed on the day following that on which Wallis joined her, and after a cruise, during which nothing eventful happened, anchored again at Bermuda on March 23rd. A little later she was joined by the 38-gun frigate *Guerriere*, Captain James Richard Dacres, and, as soon as weather permitted, both ships sailed in pursuit of two French frigates, without, however, coming up with them. On Sunday, April 26th, the ships fell in with the American schooner *Susan and Emeline*, from Bordeaux for Philadelphia, laden with cognac. She was a beautiful vessel, and sailed fast. The schooner was reported from the masthead soon after 3 p.m. Her captain looked upon the two ships as homeward-bound West Indiamen. It so happened that the courses of the schooner and the *Shannon* were such as would bring them exactly to a meeting, and neither vessel altered her course. It was dark ere the vessels neared each other, but when the schooner ascertained the mistake she had made in the character of the ships she made away under all sail. The *Shannon's* sailing powers were, however, too good for her, and coming up with the schooner about midnight, she fired two or three point-blank shots, which made the schooner shorten sail and heave to.

Such instances of the *Shannon's* exploits in capturing smaller vessels might be many times multiplied, but this will serve as an illustration for a good many of her experiences in this direction.

On May 10th the *Shannon* spoke an American vessel, and heard of the taking of Badajos by the British forces and of the raising of the siege of Cadiz, and on June 16th returned to Bermuda. Here rumours were abroad that the United States had declared war against Great Britain, and an account was received of the chase of the *Belvidera* by the U.S. ships *President* and *Congress*, under Commodore Rogers. The *Shannon* thereupon sailed for Halifax, where Captain Broke received an official intimation of the declaration of war.

All the effective ships which were then in harbour were placed under his command by Rear-Admiral Sawyer, and at once proceeded to sea, to cruise along the American coast. The squadron then consisted of the *Africa*, 64 (flag), Rear-Admiral Sir Herbert Sawyer ; the *Belvidera*, 36, Captain Richard Byron ; the *Æolus*, 32, Captain Lord James Townshend (Wallis's brother-in-law) ; and the *Shannon*. A few days later the squadron was joined by the *Guerriere*, then on her way to Halifax to refit.

Capture of U.S. Brig "Nautilus" by the "Shannon."

The squadron had not been out many days when the U.S. brig-of-war *Nautilus* was sighted, and was run down by the *Shannon* after a chase of some hours, the *Shannon* outsailing the rest of the squadron, as she frequently did when in chase.

I am content to adopt the contemporary American account of this event:—

The U.S. brig *Nautilus*, 12 guns, Captain Crane, sixteen hours from New York, on a cruise, was captured the 16*th of July* by the British frigate *Shannon*, after a chase of six hours, during which the *Nautilus* was obliged to start her water, and throw over all her lee guns. She was ordered to Halifax with Lieutenant Crane on board; the remainder of the officers and crew (106 in number) were sent on board the *Africa*.

Letter from a warrant officer of the *Nautilus* to his father:—

> " On board his Britannic Majesty's ship
> ' Africa,' at sea,
> " Lat. 37°, Long. 69°. *July 23rd*, 1812.

" Honoured Sir,—

" I have to inform you that we sailed the 15 July on a cruise. On the 16th, at sunrise, discovered five sail to windward, which proved to be British ships—*Africa, Shannon, Guerriere, Belvidera,* and *Æolus,* and which gave us chase, we then standing E. We immediately wore ship to the W., and made all sail, it then blowing fresh, and used every exertion to get clear by throwing overboard our anchors, part of our guns, and starting water in the hold—all of which proved fruitless. At half-past 12, after a chase of six hours, the *Shannon* came within half-gunshot; when we had no alternative but to strike our colours to a force so superior to ours. The officers and crew behaved like men, and would not have submitted but to a greatly superior force.

" Great praise is due to Capt. Crane for his officer and seamanlike conduct; and the lieutenants and other officers merit the attention of a grateful country.

" *Since we have been prisoners we have been treated with the utmost politeness and humanity by the officers of this ship. We have every indulgence we can expect, and can hardly realize we are prisoners.* We expect in a few days to be sent to Halifax to remain until we are exchanged, which I hope will be soon, and in the meantime our country will not forget us."

REPORT OF AMERICAN COURT-MARTIAL.

The Secretary of the Navy to Lieutenant Crane, late of the *Nautilus* :—

"NAVY DEPARTMENT, 7 *Oct.*, 1812.

"SIR,—

"The following is the opinion of the court of inquiry, convened agreeably to your request, for the loss of the U.S. brig *Nautilus :*

"The court were unanimously and decidedly in the opinion that in the capture of the late U.S. brig *Nautilus,* Lieut. Crane, her late commander, and his officers are entirely free from blame or censure ; and do consider Lieut. Crane did everything to prevent the said capture that a skilful and experienced officer could possibly do.

"This opinion of the court, Sir, only confirms the impression confidently entertained with respect to your conduct on the occasion to which it refers.

"I have the honour to be respectfully, Sir,

"Your obedient Servant,

"PAUL HAMILTON.

"WILLIAM M. CRANE, ESQ.,
"Of the Navy, Boston."

The *Nautilus,* after being sent to Halifax, was bought by the British Government, and fitted as an English sloop-of-war under the name of *Emulous,* our own *Emulous,* in which it will be remembered Wallis had served, having just then been wrecked.

It would occupy too much space, and would probably not be found very interesting, were I to describe here the numerous captures of small vessels made by the squadron, and in which Wallis took his part. It will be sufficient to state that during the first fortnight of the war the squadron burnt about forty American vessels of one sort or another, a great number being merchantmen with valuable cargoes. While the exigencies of the situation rendered it necessary that such destruction should take place, quite apart from any feeling of retaliation for similar acts on the part of the Americans, the incidents attending the burning of a ship were sometimes distressing, as the following instance will show:—An American captain had taken a fine ship to Lisbon, where she had sold her cargo for the use of the British army under Wellington, and received several thousands of dollars in return, which were on board. On her return voyage she fell a captive to the squadron, and one of the principal objects of the latter being to obtain information, the American captain was sent on board the *Shannon*, but kept in ignorance of the war, and of the fact that he was a prisoner, until the desired information had been obtained from him. He answered unreservedly the questions put to him, and Captain Broke, who greatly disliked the deception he had been obliged to practise, now felt it difficult to make the prisoner acquainted with the next step which must be taken. At length he forced himself to say: "Captain, I must burn your ship." The American, overcome by surprise, faltered: "Burn her!" "Indeed

I must." "Burn her for what? Will not money save her? She is all my own—my favourite ship, and all the property I have in the world. Is it war, then?" "Yes," replied Broke. Both parties were painfully moved, and the scene did not end without a tear from each; but the sad duty was inevitable, and the prize was destroyed.

Chase of the U.S. Frigate "Constitution."

This event has become historical in the American navy, for its length, closeness, and activity.

On July 12th, 1812, the 44-gun frigate *Constitution*, Captain Isaac Hull, completely equipped and well manned, left Chesapeake Bay bound for New York. In the afternoon of the 16th she was discovered by the British squadron, which at once gave chase. The chase continued throughout the afternoon and evening. At about 10 p.m. the *Guerriere*, which had lost sight of her companions, found the *Constitution* standing towards her making signals, and early in the morning the vessels were only half a mile apart. The other vessels of the squadron now hove in sight, but as they did not appear to understand the signals Captain Dacres made to them, he concluded they were American ships, and accordingly tacked, with the result that at daylight the distance between the *Guerriere* and the *Constitution* had so much increased, that the Captain had hopelessly lost the

chance which had presented itself of closing with the
American ship at a time when he would have been
supported by other vessels of the squadron.

At daylight there was a calm, and this continued
throughout the day. The *Constitution's* boats were
sent out to tow her head to the southward, and some
of her guns got into position. The British ships then
followed suit, and the *Constitution* having got her
head round and set sails, hoisted her colours and fired
at the *Belvidera*, which was drawing near. Some
hours later a breeze sprang up, and the *Belvidera*,
having gained on her opponent, was able to exchange
shots with her, but they were not productive of any
effect on either side. During the afternoon and night
the chase continued, the American frigate gradually
improving her position.

Throughout the following day the *Belvidera* and
Shannon, in close company, continued the chase;
but the *Constitution* increased her lead, and on the
morning of the 19th the chase was abandoned, the
Constitution having, by outsailing the enemy, escaped
a conflict which she could not have maintained with
any hope of success against a force so greatly superior.
*During this chase, which lasted sixty hours, the
whole crew remained at their stations.*

A gentleman belonging to an American captured
vessel, who was on board the *Shannon* during the
above period, has informed me that all the officers of
the British squadron applauded the conduct of Captain

Hull; and though mortified at losing so fine a ship, gave him much credit for his skill and prudence in managing the frigate. She was certainly at times in imminent danger of capture, and Captain Broke himself has recorded that the chase was a most fatiguing and anxious one, and that the *Constitution* was sailed well.

Admiral Wallis says :—" America did not declare war against us until June, when we happened to be at Halifax, also the *Africa*, 64, flagship of Sir Herbert Sawyer ; *Guerriere*, 38, Captain Dacres ; *Belvidera*, 36, Captain Byron ; and *Æolus*, 32, Captain Lord J. Townshend. The Admiral placed the squadron under the command of Broke, and we proceeded to cruise along the coast of the United States. There we fell in with the *Constitution*. On that day several sail were in sight, and we in the *Shannon* hauled up in chase of one we made out to be a man-of-war, ordering the other ships to look to the rest. We caught our bird, which turned out to be the *Nautilus*, 14 guns, Commander Crane. The wind having, on the afternoon of this day, fallen to nearly a calm, we did not rejoin our comrades until the following morning, when we found that one other of the strangers was an American frigate (to wit, *Constitution*). The *memorable chase* then began which lasted three days, with all hands at quarters, ending in her escape ; but the sad part of the tale was, the *Guerriere*, having parted company from us in foggy weather, fell in with her singly, and you know the sequel."

CAPTURE OF THE "GUERRIERE" BY THE "CONSTITUTION."

After the renowned chase just recorded the *Constitution* proceeded to Boston, but on August 2nd Captain Hull again set sail, and on the 18th received intelligence from an American privateer that she had seen a British ship to the southward, in which direction Captain Hull at once started. In the meantime Commodore Broke had fallen in with the homeward bound Jamaica fleet of sixty sail, and having escorted it over the banks of Newfoundland, stood back towards the American coast. On August 6th, or the day following, the *Guerriere*, having lost sight of Commodore Broke and his squadron in a dense fog, made for Halifax to obtain a refit—not, it would appear, before it was absolutely necessary. She had originally belonged to the French, and some time before the action which will now be recorded had been made to look smart with paint and putty; but with all her fine exterior she had scarcely a sound spar, plank, or cord about her. The mainmast had been struck by lightning, the bowsprit sprung, breechings were rotten, and timbers decayed. Notwithstanding all this, Captain Dacres seems to have had some confidence in his ship, for he had called Captain Broke's attention to her with the remark that she would take an antagonist in half the time of the *Shannon*; to which, however, Broke had replied, with a melancholy smile, "I am truly happy to hear His Majesty has so effective a ship in his service." On August 19th the *Guerriere* fell in singly with the *Constitution*, and after a severe action was captured.

The American account by Fenimore Cooper seems fair and reliable, and agrees in the main with the British :—

" The *Constitution* next stood to the southward, and on August 19th, at 2 p.m., a sail was made from the masthead. The *Constitution* immediately made sail in chase, and at three the stranger was ascertained to be a ship on the starboard tack, under easy canvas and close hauled. Half an hour later she was distinctly made out to be a frigate, and no doubt was entertained of her being an enemy. The American ship kept running free till she was within a league of the frigate and to leeward, when she began to shorten sail. By this time the enemy had laid his main-topsail aback in waiting for the *Constitution* to come down, with everything ready to engage. Perceiving that the Englishman sought a combat, Captain Hull made his own preparations with the greater deliberation. The *Constitution* consequently furled her topgallant-sails, and stowed all her light stay-sails and flying jib. Soon after she took a second reef in the topsails, hauled up the courses, sent down royal yards, cleared for action, and beat to quarters. At five the chase hoisted three English ensigns, and immediately after she opened her fire at long gunshot, wearing several times, to rake and prevent being raked. The

Constitution occasionally yawed as she approached, to avoid being raked, and she fired a few guns as they bore, but her aim was not to commence the action seriously until quite close.

"At six o'clock the enemy bore up and ran off, under his three topsails and jib, with the wind on his quarter. As this was an indication of a readiness to receive his antagonist in a fair yard-arm-and-yard-arm fight, the *Constitution* immediately set her main-top-gallant sail and fore-sail to get alongside. At a little after six, the bows of the American frigate began to double on the quarter of the English ship, when she opened with her forward guns, drawing slowly ahead with her greater way, both vessels keeping up a close and heavy fire as their guns bore. In about ten minutes, or just as the ships were fairly side by side, the mizen-mast of the Englishman was shot away, when the American passed slowly ahead, keeping up a tremendous fire, and luffed short round his bows, to prevent being raked. In executing this manœuvre, the ship shot into the wind, got sternway, and fell foul of her antagonist. While in this situation, the cabin of the *Constitution* took fire, from the close explosion of the forward guns of the enemy, who obtained a small but momentary advantage from his position. The good conduct of Mr. Hoffman,* who commanded in

---

* Beekman Verplanck Hoffman, the fourth lieutenant of the *Constitution*, a gentleman of New York, who died in 1834, a captain.

the cabin, soon repaired this accident, and a gun of
the enemy's, that threatened further injury, was
disabled.

"As the vessels touched, both parties prepared to
board. The English turned all hands up from below,
and mustered forward with that object, while Mr.
Morris, the first lieutenant, Mr. Alwyn, the master,
and Mr. Bush, the lieutenant of marines, sprang upon
the taffrail of the *Constitution* with a similar intention. Both sides now suffered by the closeness of
the musketry; the English much the most, however.
Mr. Morris was shot through the body, but maintained
his post, the bullet fortunately missing the vitals.
Mr. Alwyn was wounded in the shoulder, and Mr.
Bush fell dead, by a bullet through the head. It
being found impossible for either party to board in
the face of such a fire, and with the heavy sea that
was on, the sails were filled, and just as the *Constitution* shot ahead, the fore-mast of the enemy fell,
carrying down with it his main-mast, and leaving him
wallowing in the trough of the sea, a helpless wreck.

"The *Constitution* now hauled aboard her tacks,
ran off a short distance, secured her masts, and rove
new rigging. At seven, she wore round, and taking
a favourable position for raking, a jack that had been
kept flying on the stump of the mizen-mast of the
enemy was lowered. Mr. George Campbell Read,
the third lieutenant, was sent on board the prize, and
the boat soon returned with the report that the

captured vessel was the *Guerriere*, 38, Captain Dacres, one of the ships that had so lately chased the *Constitution*, off New York.

"The *Constitution* kept wearing, to remain near her prize, and at 2 a.m. a strange sail was seen closing, when she cleared for action; but at three the stranger stood off. At daylight the officer in charge hailed to say that the *Guerriere* had four feet of water in her hold, and that there was danger of her sinking. On receiving this information, Captain Hull sent all his boats to remove the prisoners. Fortunately, the weather was moderate, and by noon this duty was nearly ended. At 3 p.m. the prize crew was recalled, having set the wreck on fire, and in a quarter of an hour she blew up. Finding himself filled with wounded prisoners, Captain Hull now returned to Boston, where he arrived on the 30th of the same month."

Poor Dacres! one of the most genial and jocose officers on the station—he was badly wounded in the action, paroled as a prisoner of war, and most honourably acquitted by court-martial of all blame in the loss of his ship.

But I must now return to the *Shannon*, which, with her young second lieutenant, Wallis, is for a short time lying in Halifax harbour, Nova Scotia, respecting which valuable British Colony I will now say a few words.

III.

NOVA SCOTIA—FURTHER EXPLOITS OF THE "SHANNON."

CHAPTER III.

IN the great tide of emigration which so marvellously set in across the North Atlantic from Europe, during the first half of the present century, Upper and Lower Canada appear to have been most in favour.

Nova Scotia, Newfoundland, New Brunswick, Prince Edward's Island, and Cape Breton, all had separate governments in the year of which I am about to write ; but they were far less known, less sought than the Canadas—and yet Nova Scotia has produced men whose names have become renowned in British history.

In 1813 this fine British colony was thus described :—

"Nova Scotia, the most easterly province, is a peninsula connected with New Brunswick by a low

fertile isthmus. It comprises an area (with Cape
Breton Island) of 21,731 square miles, one-fifth part
of which consists of lakes, rivers, and inlets of the
sea ; of the whole extent, about 5,000,000 acres are
fit for tillage. Population of the whole province
100,000. Nova Scotia was discovered by John Cabot
in 1497 ; it was colonised by the French in 1598, and
taken by the English in 1622, and a grant made of it
by James I. to Sir William Alexander, who intended
to colonise the whole country. James I. instituted
the title of baronet there, with the professed object of
encouraging the settlement therein ; hence the title of
' Nova Scotia ' baronets. In 1632 it was restored to
France, but again ceded to England in 1714 at the
Peace of Utrecht ; after the Peace of Aix-la-Chapelle,
in 1748, a settlement of disbanded troops was formed
there by Lord Halifax, whose name the capital of the
province now bears. The harbour of Halifax is not
surpassed by any in the world. It is the principal
naval station of North America, and the British
Government have an extensive dockyard there. One-
fourth of the population are employed in agriculture.
The capabilities of the soil and climate for agricultural
operations have been much underrated. The climate
is healthy and bracing, but not so cold as the other
provinces of the dominion. The forests are composed
of similar trees to those of Canada and New Brunswick,
the ash, beech, birch, maple, oak, pine, and spruce
abounding. Coal and iron-ore are plentiful in Nova

Scotia ; gold also has been discovered. The principal fisheries are upon the eastern coast. Here cod is obtained all the year round. Halibut of large size is plentiful ; and salmon are caught abundantly in the rivers and shores adjacent thereto. Game of all kinds is abundant."

Colonial Government, 1813.

Nova Scotia.

Lieutenant-Governor and Vice-Admiral, Lieutenant-General Sir J. C. Sherbroke, *Commander of the Forces.*

Bishop, Right Rev. Chas. Inglis, D.D.

Chief-Justice, S. Salter Blowers, Esq.

Second Judge, J. H. Monk, Esq.

Third Judge, Brenton Haliburton, Esq.

Attorney-General, R. J. Uniacke, Esq.

Solicitor-General, J. Stewart, Esq.

Prothonotary and Clerk of the Crown, W. Thomson, Esq.

Secretary of the Provincial Records and Clerk of the Council, S. H. George.

Treasurer, M. Wallace.

Surveyor of Lands, C. Morris.

Naval Officer, J. Beckwith.

Collector of Customs at Halifax, T. Jeffery.

Comptroller, J. Slayter.

Departmental Paymaster, G. J. Williams.

Surveyor and Searcher, J. Newton.

Judge of the Vice-Admiralty Court, Alex. Croke, D.C.L.

Registrar of Vice-Admiralty Court, T. H. Parker.

Marshal, J. Putman.

Agent, T. J. Matthias, *King's College,* 1802.

Governors, Sir J. Wentworth, Bart., Bishop of Nova Scotia, S. S. Blowers, Esq., R. J. Uniacke, Esq., Jas. Stewart, Esq.

Patron, Archbishop of Canterbury.

Visitor, Bishop of Nova Scotia.

President, Rev. Thomas Porter.

Names all more or less intimately connected with
the events of the war between Great Britain and the
United States. All thoroughly loyal to the British
Government. Many, no doubt, of their descendants,
scanning that list, will pause at some one name and
think, with proper pride—"*I bear it still. His
sentiments are mine!*"

Nova Scotia has given birth to Beckwith, of
Waterloo; Williams, of Kars; Inglis, of Lucknow;
Watts and Belcher, of Arctic fame, and other eminent men; but to none more so than the illustrious
subject of this memoir, and the witty "Sam Slick,"
properly Thomas C. Haliburton, afterwards Chief-
Justice of that colony, who in age was five years
younger than Wallis, and of whom I shall have to
speak at greater length hereafter. He was a son
of Judge Brenton Haliburton, and at this time a
youthful subaltern in the British army, a profession
he afterwards relinquished for the law.

CHASE OF THE "ESSEX."

The *Shannon* continued on her cruising ground,
and after having made several unimportant captures,
fell in, on September 4th, with the American frigate
Essex, Captain Porter, and the merchant ship
Minerva, which was under her convoy. The
Shannon at once gave chase under all sail, but the
wind making a sudden and unfavourable change

headed her back. The *Essex*, however, seemed inclined to bring the *Shannon* to action, and got nearer to her, with the *Minerva* in close company; then suddenly changed her course, and crowding on all sail, made off, leaving the *Minerva* to take care of herself. The *Shannon* kept up the chase until dark, when, losing sight of the *Essex*, she tacked and captured the *Minerva*, which vessel Captain Broke would have at once burnt, in the hope that the *Essex* might see the flames and return to have revenge, had not the night been so squally, that the *Shannon's* boats would have been risked in removing the *Minerva's* crew. It was not until morning, therefore, that the *Minerva* was burnt, and by this time the *Essex* had been able to get out of reach. About a fortnight after, the *Shannon* returned to Halifax with some prizes, and there heard the melancholy news of the loss of the *Guerriere*.

Having on October 3rd learnt that the *Barbadoes* had been wrecked on Sable Island, the *Shannon* on that day sailed to her relief, and after considerable difficulty succeeded in saving the crew of 180 and a good deal of specie. A few days later an American schooner was captured, and manned with a part of the crew taken from the wrecked vessel, and Halifax again reached. Then, in company with the *Tenedos*, 38, Captain Hyde Parker, *Nymph*, and *Curlew*, the *Shannon* once more set sail, and captured, among numerous other vessels, the American privateer *Thorn*, 18 guns and 140 men, ultimately beating into Halifax again on February 23rd, 1813.   Not for long, however, could the *Shannon* afford to lay in harbour, and in company with the *Tenedos* she was soon reconnoitring Boston Harbour.   At about this period, viz., on April 5th, the *Shannon* had a narrow escape, which Captain Broke thus records :—

" On the evening of the 5th, at half-past eight, we were struck with lightning when laying to, boarding a small schooner we had taken ; the main-top-mast and top-gallant-mast shivered to pieces, and fifteen feet out of the middle of the former blown to atoms ; the topsail yard broke in the slings, a cheek and hasp forced off the head of the mainmast, and the mast much shook to the quarterdeck, where the partners were broke.   The mainyard sprung in two places; the brass skewers in the truck melted as if they had been in a furnace, also some of the links of the maintop chain.   Fire was in the top for some seconds after the crash, and nothing but the heavy rain and the goodness of Providence saved us from destruction ; and, thanks be to God, not a man was hurt.   I was in the cabin at the moment, when I thought several of the guns had been fired.   When I ran on deck I still saw fire in the top.   Those on board the schooner close astern of us thought we were in a blaze."

About a month later the *Shannon* and *Tenedos* espied an armed ship under American colours, and chased her on shore near Cape Anne. Then having dispersed the militia, which was assembling to protect her, the boats of the two British ships were sent in under the command of Wallis, who brought the vessel off. She proved to be *L'Invincible*, a French privateer of 16 guns, then lately captured by H.M. sloop *Mutine* and retaken by an American privateer.

I have followed the doings of the *Shannon* somewhat minutely, as from them will be gathered the experiences which fell to the lot of Wallis during these early days of his career. It will be seen that up to this time he had been almost continually in the midst of the many dangers attending naval warfare, as well as braving the elements, which, I think I am right in saying, were far more destructive to the old sailing ships than to our modern steamers. I would add that the station on which Wallis was engaged was a most trying one. It was no uncommon thing for the *Shannon* to be a mass of ice from stem to stern; the spray froze on her guns and deck as it fell; sails became as brittle as glass; ropes cracked when moved, and fingers became frost-bitten in handling them; the weather was indeed so inclement that the *Shannon's* crew were at times obliged to wear thick worsted underdresses, mittens, and Welsh wigs.

Wallis was now to take his part in one of the most

sanguinary conflicts that are recorded in our naval history ; but before giving an account of this, it will be well to a little more fully describe the character of the gallant commander of the *Shannon*, and also some of the measures he took to be in readiness to carry his ship successfully into action with a foe of at least equal strength, should good fortune give him the opportunity.

He was an unusually able disciplinarian and skilful sailor, and, by his excellent regulations and mode of treatment, the somewhat motley ship's company which he had taken on board some years previously had been trained so thoroughly, and had become so well acquainted with him, that they had now reached a high degree of efficiency. Broke was himself a most proficient gunner, and discovered and made use of an ingenious mode of laying ships' ordnance, which afterwards received the highest commendation. He also established a system of exercises with the great guns and small arms, which were carried out assiduously and with great regularity whenever the state of the weather permitted and the crew were not engaged in active duties, such as those necessitated by a chase. It may be remarked that one feature of these exercises was that those men who would have to *fight* together in the time of action were *exercised* together. Some small reward was frequently given to a successful competitor, and the men were made to enjoy these practices, and to take pride in their own proficiency. Add to this that Broke watched over his crew and young officers, whom he called his *sea-children*, with a parental care, and, as he himself says, regarded the bringing up of such a family as an essential part of his service, it is not to be wondered at that he was beloved by his men, and that perfect unanimity prevailed on board. He was proud, too, of his *wooden wife*, as he sometimes called his ship, and, with his crew, ardently longed to try her with one of the American frigates, and to redeem his country's reputation, which it was now the boast of the Americans had been lost with the *Guerriere* and other vessels which had fallen captive to their ships, albeit the latter were in all these cases of superior size and power.

Such was the condition of things on board the *Shannon* immediately prior to the happening of those events which I will now record.

IV.

THE BLOCKADE OF BOSTON, AND CAPTURE OF THE "CHESAPEAKE."

CAPTAIN LAWRENCE,

COMMANDER OF THE U. S. FRIGATE "CHESAPEAKE."

CHAPTER IV.

NAVAL matters were now hastening to a crisis. All the eastern American ports were strictly watched, that of Boston by the *Shannon* and *Tenedos* ; and an arduous time indeed they had of it, throughout the months of April and May 1813. Foggy, very foggy weather, even for these latitudes, prevailed ; and under veil of one of those friendly allies, the *President* and *Congress* stole past their guard, out to sea, and so escaped, much to the annoyance of Captain Broke, who during his long and diligent watch had been hourly hoping that these formidable American frigates would turn out to fight. The *Chesapeake* alone, fit for action, remained in harbour ; and Broke, who only desired to meet the enemy singly, fairly, and with a decisive result, at once challenged her commander, the brave Lawrence, in the following courteous letter :—

"H.B.M. 'SHANNON,' OFF BOSTON,
"*June*, 1813.

" SIR,—

" As the *Chesapeake* appears now ready for sea, I request that you will do me the favour to meet the *Shannon* with her, ship to ship, to try the fortune of our respective flags. To an officer of your character, it requires some apology for proceeding to further particulars. Be assured, sir, that it is not from any doubt I can entertain of your wishing to close with my proposal, but merely to provide an answer to any objection which might be made, and very reasonably, upon the chance of our receiving unfair support. After the diligent attention which we had paid to Commodore Rogers, the pains I took to detach all force but the *Shannon* and *Tenedos* to such a distance that they could not possibly join in any action fought in sight of the Capes, and the various verbal messages which had been sent into Boston to that effect, we were much disappointed to find the Commodore had eluded us by sailing on the first change, after the prevailing easterly winds had obliged us to keep an offing from the coast. He, perhaps, wished for some stronger assurance of a fair meeting. I am, therefore, induced to address you more particularly, and to assure you that what I write I pledge my honour to perform to the utmost of my power. The *Shannon* mounts 24 guns upon her broadside, and 1 light boat gun ; 18-pounders upon her maindeck, and 32-pound carronades on her quarterdeck and forecastle; and is manned with a complement of 300 men and boys (a large proportion of the latter), besides 30 seamen, boys, and passengers, who were taken out of recaptured vessels lately. I am thus minute, because a report has prevailed in some of the Boston papers that we had 150 men additional, lent us from *La Hogue*, which really never was the case. *La Hogue* is now gone to Halifax for provisions, and I will send all other ships beyond the power of interfering with us, and meet you wherever it is most agreeable to you, within the limits of the undermentioned rendezvous, viz., from six to ten leagues east of Cape Cod lighthouse; from eight to ten leagues east of Cape Ann's light; on Cashe's Ledge, in latitude 43° north; at any bearing and distance you please to fix, off the south breakers of Nantucket, or the shoal of St. George's Bank. If you will favour me with any plan of signals or telegraph, I will warn you (if sailing under this promise) should any of my friends be too nigh, or anywhere in sight, until I can detach them out of my way; or I would sail with you, under a flag of truce, to any place you think safest from our cruisers, hauling it down when fair to begin hostilities.

"You must, sir, be aware that my proposals are highly advantageous to you, as you cannot proceed to sea singly in the *Chesapeake* without imminent risk of being crushed by the superior force of the numerous British squadrons which are now abroad, where all

4

your efforts, in case of a *rencontre*, would, however gallant, be perfectly hopeless. I entreat you, sir, not to imagine that I am urged by mere personal vanity to the wish of meeting the *Chesapeake*, or that I depend only upon your personal ambition for your acceding to this invitation. We have both nobler motives.

" You will feel it as a compliment if I say that the result of our meeting may be the most grateful service I can render to my country; and I doubt not that you, equally confident of success, will feel convinced that it is only by repeated triumphs, in even combats, that your little navy can now hope to console your country for the loss of that trade it can no longer protect. Favour me with a speedy reply. We are short of provisions and water, and cannot stay long here.

" I have the honour to be, Sir,

" Your obedient, humble servant,

" P. B. V. BROKE,

" Captain of H.B.M. *Shannon*.

" N.B.—For the general service of watching your coast, it is requisite for me to keep another ship in company to support me with her guns and boats when employed near the land, and particularly to aid each other if either ship, in chase, should get on shore. You must be aware that I cannot, consistently with my duty, waive so great an advantage for this general service, by detaching my consort without an assurance on your part of meeting me directly, and that you will neither seek nor admit aid from any other of your armed vessels if I despatch mine expressly for the sake of meeting you. Should any special order restrain you from thus answering a formal challenge, you may yet oblige me by keeping my proposal a secret, and appointing any place you like to meet us (within 300 miles of Boston) in a given number of days after you sail ; as, unless you agree to an interview, I may be busied on other service, and, perhaps, be at a distance from Boston when you go to sea.

" Choose your terms, but let us meet.

" To the Commander of the
        " U.S. frigate *Chesapeake*."

In order that Captain Lawrence might be assured that the Captain of the *Shannon* only desired a fair contest, the latter had detached his consort, the *Tenedos*, with orders not to rejoin him until the end of June, and remained cruising singly off the Capes.

Anxious to secure a competent judgment on my own account of the action which speedily followed the above challenge, I submitted it to the opinion of the late Admiral Lord Dunsany, who replied thus :—

" All that I read of Sir P. Broke pleased me much, and the battle, read aloud one evening, stirred us all up to fighting pitch. It is certainly by far the fullest and most accurate record of that interesting event I have ever seen."

This account now follows :—

War is always to be deprecated—always, if possible, to be avoided—and it will be no object in the present volume to excite a thirst for glory in the young. But, at the same time, it will be desired to commend (by signal examples) the honour which always follows the discharge of *duty* in our appointed stations in life ; of loyalty to our country and its rulers, and of submission to that Divine Power at Whose supreme disposal are the issues of all earthly events.

Philip Bowes Vere Broke was one in whom, it may be truly said, these principles grew with his growth, strengthened with his strength, and increased with his advancing years—even to their close.

Though, like his contemporaries, a gallant sailor, he was also a man of very superior intellectual attainments ; a classical scholar of refined perceptions, a thorough officer, not only respected but sincerely beloved by those he commanded ; whilst in private life, as husband, father, and friend, he was long mourned by those who in these respects were privileged to know him.

Such was the captain who trained our hero ; nor was his scholar unworthy of him, as we shall see.

The morning of that most eventful day, Tuesday, June 1st, 1813, broke over the shores and islands of the Bay of Boston in unclouded summer loveliness. A faint breeze rippled the waters, and the rising sun cast long rays of light and broken brilliancy over the wide and gently heaving bosom of the Bay. The *Shannon*, under easy sail, slowly floated down the eastern coast, in order to take an early look into the harbour and upon the vessels of the enemy. Viewed from seaward, a more peaceful scene could scarcely be conceived. The lighthouse, friendly alike to friend and foe, the distant shore, the light hazy clouds over the port and town of Boston, and the lofty masts and widespread spars of the man-of-war lying ready for sea—these, as usual, were the prominent objects on which the eager and anxious gaze of Broke had often before rested. But to-day, or at furthest to-morrow, he had strong hopes the issue would be decided. His challenge, that model of the utterance of a bravery which had well calculated and was now resolute to stand the hazard of the die, had gone forth.

Meanwhile all went on as usual on board the well-ordered, well-trained, unassuming, and well-disciplined *Shannon*. At eight bells a.m. the gallant young Wallis took the watch ; and from that hour onward to the close, the events of this momentous day are all within the accurate reach and record of the historian's pen, employed only on facts furnished by eye-witnesses of the engagement. The previous day had been rainy, and there were consequently many small matters of watchful routine and ever-ready preparedness requiring attention. At 10 a.m., these duties being discharged, the beat to quarters rattled along the decks, and sent its short, sharp, and alert summons down the hatchways of the *Shannon*. Quickly, silently, and resolutely the men repaired to their appointed stations, and the great gun exercise, without firing, was assiduously practised as the British frigate, with light airs of wind, made quiet reaches to and fro across the bay, full in the enemy's sight.

It was at this time that the vigilant captain, in the prime of his manhood and the calm of his settled purpose to conquer or die for his country's honour, ascended to the *Shannon's* maintop. Until half-past eleven he remained there, watching eagerly the tapering masts and widespread yards of the beleagured ship, which, beyond a loose foretopsail, gave no sign of her departure. Slowly, and deeply disappointed, Broke descended to the deck and ordered the retreat from quarters, observing to his young officer: "Wallis, I don't mean this for general quarters, but because she (with a gesture towards. the harbour) will surely be out to-day or to-morrow." The watch was relieved, and the young lieutenant said cheerily to his successor, as he went below, " Be sure you call me if she stir." The men went to dinner. Broke lingered still on deck, for the tide was flowing and the day already beginning to wane.

It was the gallant Falkiner's watch, and he is now not here to give us the precise details; but in that quiet hour of rest, from the meridian eight bells, the word passed on lightning wings along the decks—

"She is coming out," and soon every *Shannon's* eye was on her movements. At length the watch and ward of weary, toilsome weeks was ended. Sail after sail spread forth, flag after flag unfurled, and with all the speed the light air and an ebbing tide could yield her, and attended by a large number of lesser craft to witness and applaud her expected triumph, the haughty *Chesapeake* bore down upon her waiting adversary. Her commander, Lawrence, glowing with recent triumph, anticipated an easy victory. Colossal in figure, and with muscular power superior to most men, he was on this day fatally conspicuous by the white vest and other habiliments he had assumed. Having stimulated his men to the utmost by prize cheques and an exciting harangue, closing with the sanguinary and remorseless words— "Peacock her, my lads! Peacock her!"* he then ascended to his quarterdeck, with the full determination of forthwith wreaking the like speedy destruction on the *Shannon*. His words, however, had fallen on irresponsive and misgiving hearts. There was murmuring forward and depressing caution aft. The men were discontented, and American officers, not of the *Chesapeake* (but who accompanied Lawrence, and his two youthful sons to the wharf, from which he was to pull on board his ship), had whispered: "Be

---

* On the previous 24th of February, Lawrence, in the *Hornet*, had sunk the British brig-of-war *Peacock*, of eighteen guns, in little more than fifteen minutes.

cautious; take heed. We know every British ship on the station but this *Shannon*."

Far different was it on board "this *Shannon*," rusty with long cruising, her ensign faded and worn (she wore but one), and short of provisions and water.

The moment, the long-desired moment of reckoning, was at hand; and but one feeling prevailed on board,—to exact it to the utmost.

Broke (amid the busy hum of interest on the quarterdeck) descended silently and thoughtfully to his cabin, and there made his own final personal arrangements. What passed in that solemn hour no living creature now on earth can tell; but we know enough of the warrior to feel assured that he then committed himself, and the wife and children then probably sleeping the sleep of the peaceful in distant England, to the great God he had so long confessed and honoured.

The battle-ground, some fifteen or twenty miles from Boston, being very nearly reached, the men were at once called aft, and their commander proceeded to address them. He stood on the break of the quarterdeck, the men of the upper-deck quarters standing in front of him and along the gangways; the men of the maindeck assembled below, and within partial earshot. In substance, Broke addressed them thus:—

"*Shannons!* You know that, from various causes, the Americans have lately triumphed, on several occasions, over the British flag in our frigates. This will not daunt you since you know the truth, that disparity of force was the chief reason. But they have gone further : they have said, and they have published it in their papers, that the English have forgotten the way to fight. You will let them know to-day there are Englishmen in the *Shannon* who still know how to fight. Don't try to dismast her. Fire into her quarters ; maindeck into maindeck ; quarterdeck into quarterdeck. Kill the men and the ship is yours. Don't hit them about the head, for they have steel caps on, but give it them through the body. Don't cheer. Go quietly to your quarters. I feel sure you will all do your duty ; and remember, you have now the blood of hundreds of your countrymen to avenge ! "

At this stirring and touching allusion to the fate of the *Guerriere,* the *Macedonian,* and the *Java,** many of the hardy seamen wept. A dead and heavy silence (the voiceless calm of do or die) rested over the *Shannon's* decks ; but it was twice broken before a shot was fired. Jacob West, late of the *Guerriere,* said : "I hope, sir, you will give us revenge for the *Guerriere* to-day." To which Broke replied, " You shall have it, my man ; go to your quarters." Another

---

* I have already recorded the loss of the *Guerriere.* The *Macedonian* was captured by the American frigate *United States,* and the *Java* by the *Constitution.* It may be added that the *Java,* like the *Guerriere,* had been taken from the French.

seaman, eyeing the rusty blue ensign which fluttered at the *Shannon's* mizen peak, asked : " Mayn't we have three ensigns, sir, like she has ? "   " No," said Broke, " we've always been an unassuming ship."

All now went silently and resolutely to their stations.

At this moment, all being ready for action, Boston light bearing west, distant about six leagues, the *Shannon* finally hauled up, with her head to the southward and eastward, and lay-to under topsails and jib, the latter flowing and the spanker hanging by the throatbrail only, ready for wearing or running free, and the helm amidships.

The *Chesapeake* was now coming rapidly down, at an angle of impunity, having sent her royal yards on deck and reduced her sail to very much the same dimensions as her adversary. The *Shannon's* royal yards were kept across, as her captain considered that those lofty sails might be serviceable in the event of the light air dying away, or being altogether lulled by the approaching cannonade.

When nearly within gunshot the *Shannon* filled under jib, topsails, and spanker, and, having little more than steerage way, awaited her opponent's closer approach. All were now at their posts. On the quarterdeck Broke, assisted by his first lieutenant, Watt, and attended by his aide-de-camp, Mr. Fenn (a light-hearted midshipman and general favourite on board, more familiarly known as Tommy Fenn), and the marine officers. The purser (a volunteer), the clerk, and a trusty sergeant (Molyneux) were stationed in the waist and gangways. The maindeck was most ably officered by Wallis and Falkiner, the former being in command of the after batteries, which it is perhaps needless to say were fought with bravery and skill. Before a shot was fired, and as the men were going to quarters, Meehan, the gunner, was on his way to the magazine, when Wallis arrested him for a moment, and handed to him his watch, saying, "You will be safe. Should anything happen to me give this to my father with my love." By this chronometer the gunner timed the action.

It was at first doubtful whether the *Chesapeake* would make a raking evolution astern of the *Shannon*, or come fairly alongside; but when she arrived within pistol-shot all suspense was ended, for she rounded-to on the starboard quarter of her opponent—precisely the *Hornet's* mode of attack when, with her, Lawrence captured the *Peacock*.

Captain Broke walked forward, and through his own skylight gave orders to the maindeck captains of guns to "fire on the enemy as soon as the guns bore on his second bow-port." (A man named Rowlands, who was captain of the maintop on board the *Guerriere* when captured by the *Constitution*, was so delighted by this order that he very audibly and admiringly ejaculated: "Ah! that's the man for me; she's ours!") Broke now walked forward to the starboard gangway to observe the effect of his directions. The ships were

closing fast. The sails of the *Chesapeake* came
gliding between the slanting rays of the evening
sun and the *Shannon,* darkening the maindeck ports
of the latter, whilst the increasing ripple of the water
against her bows as she approached could be distinctly
heard at all the guns of the after-battery on the
Shannon's silent maindeck.   In another moment, the
desired position being attained, the *Shannon* commenced the action by firing her after or fourteenth
maindeck gun ; the steady old captain of the gun,
Billy Mindham (Captain Broke's faithful coxswain),
having first reported to Wallis, the officer of his
quarters, that his gun bore, and received permission
to fire ; a second afterwards, her after-carronade on
the quarterdeck ; then her thirteenth maindeck gun ;
and, as the *Chesapeake* ranged alongside, she received,
in close and steady succession, the whole of the broadside. The effect of this (as witnessed from the
Shannon's tops) was truly withering. A hurricane of
shot, splinters, torn hammocks, cut rigging, and wreck
of every kind was hurled like a cloud across the deck.
Of 150 men quartered thereon more than 100 were
instantly laid low. Nor was this all. In this moment
of deadly strife, Lawrence, who was fatally conspicuous,
standing on a carronade-slide, received a ball through
his abdomen from the hand of Lieut. Law, of the
marines. He fell, severely wounded, and, after four
days of suffering, doomed to die. But to relate this
at present is premature. The conflict continued. In

THE AMERICAN FRIGATE "CHESAPEAKE"

CRIPPLED AND THROWN INTO UTTER DISORDER BY THE TWO FIRST BROADSIDES FIRED FROM
H.M.S. "SHANNON."

passing the *Shannon*, and after receiving her first
broadside, the *Chesapeake* made a stern board; her
tiller ropes and jib-sheet had been shot away, her
wheel broken; and thus she gradually luffed into the
wind, exposed, whilst making this crippled and helpless movement, to the *Shannon's* second and most
deliberate broadside. From the first the *Chesapeake*
had apparently attached much importance to her
small-arm force, with which indeed, from her tops
and deck, she commenced the action. It was now
the *Shannon's* turn and time to make use of these.
Broke saw that she was crippled, and, by his order,
the marines in the gangways and the seamen in the
boats and clustering about the booms, under the direction of Aldham, Dunn, and Molyneux, poured in a
precise and deliberate fire. Broke perceived the
flinching of the enemy, and, throwing down his
trumpet, hurried forward with the simple words,
" Follow me who can !" The *Chesapeake* had continued drifting astern till her larboard quarter struck
the *Shannon* about the fifth or sixth gun on the maindeck. Here the veteran boatswain, Mr. Stevens, who
had fought in Rodney's action, received, in lashing
the ships together, the wounds of which he afterwards
died in hospital at Halifax.

The ships were in contact at but a small point, and
but for a short time. Fifty or sixty gallant hearts,
however, had fortunately heard their brave captain's
words, and followed him closely. Lieutenants Watt

and Falkiner, Collier, Stack, Van Loo, Fish (first and second gunners), and others, stationed chiefly on the quarterdeck, with a large body of marines, pressed on in the way so nobly led by their captain.   On gaining the *Chesapeake's* deck, a desperate and disorderly resistance was made.   Her so-called chaplain, a Mr. Livermore, of Boston (an amateur and volunteer, no more), presented and snapped a pistol at Captain Broke.   A backward stroke of the good and weighty Toledo blade which the hero carried (mounted, however, in the regulation ivory and gold wire) left his reverence to his better meditations against the mizenmast; and a vigorous charge along the gangways followed.   This was the most confused moment of the conflict.   A severe encounter had been raging in the tops.   The midshipmen — Smith in the fore and Cosnahan in the main—had vastly distinguished themselves.   Smith boarded the enemy off the fore-yard of the *Shannon*, and, after hard fighting, chased his last remaining adversary down the foretopmast backstay on to the deck.   Cosnahan, in the maintop, finding the foot of the topsail intervene between the enemy and himself, laid out on the manyardarm, and, receiving loaded muskets handed down to him through the "lubber's hole," shot three men from thence.   These were midshipmen indeed!

To add to the confusion, the *Chesapeake's* head gradually falling off, her sails again filled; she broke away from the lashings, and forged across the bow of

H.M.S. "SHANNON"

CARRYING BY BOARDING THE AMERICAN FRIGATE "CHESAPEAKE," AFTER A CANNONADE
OF FIVE MINUTES.

the *Shannon*. At this moment, it would appear, the
English party had divided — the upper deck was
entirely theirs; Watt was aft, hauling down the
enemy's flag. Broke was on the forecastle, inter-
posing between his men and some three or four
Americans, who must otherwise have instantly been
cut to pieces. The first lieutenant, in his haste—
unwisely, alas! we can now see—hurrying the sailors
so employed, caused them to bend on a white ensign
under the American ensign.* The moment this was
seen from the *Shannon* her fire recommenced, and a
grape-shot from his own ship carried away the top of
his head, the same discharge killing and wounding
others around him. The consternation diffused by
this accident on the *Chesapeake's* quarterdeck
reanimated the conquered Americans on the forecastle. Broke had already spared their lives—that
was nothing. With pike, sabre, and musket they
formed *behind* their gallant preserver; and when,
roused by a fervent adjuration from a sentinel, he

* Edward Rexworthy was one of the *Shannon's* quartermasters;
he was standing before Lieut. Watt when the grape-shot from the
Shannon's seventh gun, maindeck, passed over Rexworthy's head and
pierced Watt's chest—Rexworthy was a very short man, Lieut. Watt
was six feet, or rather more. Whenever the *Shannon* beat to quarters
in expectation of a battle, Lieut. Watt always had a white ensign laid
upon the capstan; and this, he said, was "to hoist over the colours
of the enemy." He boarded with this in his hand; and there is no
doubt about its having been hoisted up some distance *under*, instead
of *over*, the American ensign on board the *Chesapeake*. It was this
mistake, as every one said at the time, which caused the seventh gun
to be fired at that party.

unsuspectingly turned about, he found not one, nor two, but three men—but, no! let me rather say, treacherous, indomitable enemies — prepared and anxious to take his life. These were great odds; but Broke parried the pike of his first assailant and wounded him in the face. Before he could recover his guard, the second foe struck him with a cutlass on the side of the head; and, instantly on this, the third having clubbed his musket drove home his comrade's weapon, until a large surface of the skull was cloven entirely away—the brain was left bare. Broke sank, of necessity, stunned and bleeding, on the deck; his sword fell from his relaxing grasp, and his first assailant, who had already fallen, strove to muster sufficient strength to consummate the attack. At this moment a marine bayoneted the immediate opponent of his captain, whilst the enraged *Shannons* almost literally cut his companions to pieces. It was truly a sanguinary scene. Broke was scarcely to be recognised, even by his own comrades. He was plastered with lime and blood.* Mr. Smith and Mindham, however, tenderly raised him; and, whilst the latter bound an old handkerchief round his captain's streaming head, he applied a strong mental cordial by directing his look aft, with the cheering words: "Look there, sir; there goes the old ensign up over the Yankee colours!"

---

* The Americans had an open cask of lime to throw in the eyes of the boarders. This was shattered by one of the *Shannon's* shot.

TREACHEROUS ATTACK ON CAPTAIN BROKE,

BY THREE OF THE "CHESAPEAKE'S" MEN, ON HER FORECASTLE.

Page 74.

Slowly they then led him to the quarterdeck, and seated him, half fainting, on a carronade-slide.

Whilst these events were passing on the *Chesapeake's* forecastle and quarterdeck, an animated conflict had been going forward (for not more than two minutes, however) on her maindeck. This also ended in the dispersion of her crew. They were driven below, a grating placed over the main hatch-way, and a marine (William Young) posted sentry over it. It chanced that this man, seeing a comrade pass, stretched out his hand by way of congratulation on their victory and joint escape. Whilst doing this he was most treacherously shot from below. The surrounding *Shannons*, terribly enraged, instantly poured down among the Americans a warm discharge of musketry. This proceeding excited the anger of the brave Lieutenant Falkiner, who was sitting on the booms, fatigued by his exertions in boarding. He rushed forward, and, presenting his pistol, pro-tested he would blow out the brains of the first man who attempted to fire another shot. He then sang out to the Americans below that, if they did not instantly send up the man who shot the marine, he would call them up and put them to death one by one. This vigorous proceeding put an end to all further resistance.

The firing alluded to aroused Broke, and, on being informed of the cause, he faintly directed the

5

Americans to be driven into the hold, and then lapsed, from his great loss of blood, into total insensibility.

The battle was now over and the victory won, according to the most careful and largest computation of time, in thirteen minutes. In this brief space 252 men were either killed or wounded in the two ships, the loss of the Americans being about 70 killed and 100 wounded, and that of the English 26 killed and 56 wounded. Fresh reinforcements of *Shannons* were now sent on board the *Chesapeake*, the boats conveying back to the English ship her gallant Captain Broke, and the first lieutenant of the enemy (Augustus Ludlow), both severely, and the latter, as it turned out, mortally wounded. Captain Broke was laid in his own cot, in his own cabin, his "good old sword" ("Pray," said he, "take care of my good old sword") being laid beside him. Lieutenant Ludlow (who, in the hurry of the moment, was left for a little while lying unnoticed in the steerage) sent a touching message— "Will you tell the commanding officer of the *Shannon* that Mr. Ludlow, first of the *Chesapeake*, is lying here badly wounded?" He was immediately placed in the berth of poor Watt. And Captain Lawrence, who, on receiving his wound had been conveyed, in consequence of the shattered state of his cabin, to the *Chesapeake's* wardroom, remained there—in four

days to breathe his last. The Americans, in full
confidence of victory, had provided several hundred
pairs of handcuffs for the English. "With their
own" (as Admiral Wallis quaintly remarks) "they
were now ornamented."

At this moment the ships were lying not, perhaps,
more than pistol-shot asunder, with their heads
towards the eastward. The action was over. The
companion vessels of the *Chesapeake* slowly and
sadly steered back to Boston. The sun went down
over the blood-stained waters of the bay; and in the
twilight interval between his setting and the moon's
uprising, which that night lighted the British the
first stage of their triumphant voyage to Halifax,
the slain were committed to the deep—in the sublime
language of the Church of England Liturgy, "to
be turned into corruption, looking for the resurrection of the body, when the sea shall give up her
dead"—tenderly, yet quickly; sadly, and with few
words. This done, the rigging was knotted, the
masts fished, and the decks partially washed. The
Shannons then divided. Half of her choicest
officers—Falkiner, Smith, Raymond, Leake, and
Johns—going on board the prize; the rest, with
their now unconscious captain, remaining on board
the *Shannon*. So, full in sight of hundreds of
Americans thronging the highlands of Gloucester
and Cape Anne, the two ships, having shaped their
course for Halifax, slowly receded from the land,

and from the sight of the afflicted inhabitants of Boston.

Before proceeding to relate a few anecdotes of the action, I propose to give a short extract from the *American* report of the court-martial on the loss of their frigate, which concludes thus:—

"This court respectfully begs leave to superadd, that, unbiassed by any illiberal feeling towards the enemy, they feel it their duty to state, that the conduct of the enemy, after boarding and carrying the *Chesapeake*, was a most unwarrantable abuse of power after success.

"The court is aware that in carrying a ship by boarding, the full extent of the command of an officer cannot be readily exercised, and that improper violence may unavoidably ensue. When this happens in the moment of contention, a magnanimous conquered foe will not complain. But the fact has been clearly established before this court, that the enemy met with little opposition on the upper deck, and none on the gun-deck. Yet, after they had carried the ship, they fired from the gun-deck down the hatchway upon the berth-deck, and killed and wounded several of the *Chesapeake's* crew, who had retreated there, were unarmed and incapable of making any opposition; that some balls were fired even into the cockpit; and what excites the utmost abhorrence, this outrage was committed in the presence of a British officer standing at the hatchway.

"W. BAINBRIDGE, *President.*"

The incident referred to here was undoubtedly a painful one, but it is only necessary to call the reader's attention to the actual and unquestionable facts, as stated on p. 75 of this present volume, to show how grossly it has been misrepresented in the American account just given.

ANECDOTES OF THE ACTION.

Between three and four o'clock in the afternoon of this 1st of June, the officers of the *Shannon* bivouacked for their last dinner on the quarterdeck. The cabins were cleared away for action, the ship was standing out to sea, a screen of canvas had been run up and the commissioned officers invited to join their captain at his improvised table. There had been some slight misunderstanding and consequent coolness between two of his lieutenants which had pained Broke much, and he embraced the opportunity of reconciling them. Those were the good old days of taking wine with each other, in token of mutual friendship. When the cloth was cleared away, and before the wine was removed, Broke rose and thus addressed his guests : " Well, gentlemen, no

doubt we shall shortly be in action. It will be a satisfaction to me if we all take wine with each other,
and shake hands all round, before we go to quarters."
As this custom of " taking wine " has quite gone
out of use, except among the few survivors of the
first quarter of the present century, I may mention
that it was considered a mark of especial regard
and friendship; and many are the quarrels, both
in the army and navy, which have been at once
prevented by this simple formula, *e.g.*—

Admiral W. : " Captain Jones, a glass of wine ? "
Captain J. : " I shall feel honoured, Admiral."
Admiral W. : " Will you join us, Captain Davis ? "
Captain D. : " With the greatest pleasure, sir."

And then the parties simultaneously raised their
glasses, bowed, and smiling graciously to each
other, drained them, and J. and D. became friends
again. So was it on board the *Shannon* about four
hours only before the death of one of the officers
thus reconciled.

This action on the part of Captain Broke is
almost parallel with that of Nelson at the battle of
Trafalgar, related in Southey's Life, and his description of which it will be convenient to repeat. Admiral
Collingwood had gone on board the *Victory* with
some of the captains to receive instructions, when
Nelson inquired of him where his captain was.
Collingwood, in reply, said : " We are not upon good
terms with each other." " Terms ! " said Nelson,

"good terms with each other!" and immediately sent a boat for Captain Rotherham. As soon as he arrived Nelson led him to Collingwood, saying, "Look! yonder are the enemy!" and bade them shake hands like Englishmen.

As an instance of presence of mind it is related that, after Captain Broke had been laid low from the effect of the wounds inflicted upon him, one of his antagonists, who had fallen by his side, made a final effort to kill Broke outright, and managed to get uppermost in a faint struggle. He had in his hand a bayonet, and his arm was outstretched ready to strike, when one of the *Shannon's* marines, John Hill, drew near. He did not, however, recognise friend from foe ; and, thinking that the enemy *must* be the man who was undermost, was about to thrust his bayonet into his own commander, when the latter said, "Pooh, you fool ! don't you know your captain ? " The next second Hill had made his thrust, but it was through the American.

The brave but unfortunate Lawrence, while being carried to the wardroom of the *Chesapeake*, mortally wounded, said, " Don't give up the ship," and it would appear that he repeated these words when delirious from his wounds. He was gentle and docile during the few days that were left to him, and fully anticipated his fate, which he met with the quiet resignation of a brave man. He had behaved most humanely to captive foes, and his worth and gallantry have never found a detractor in any British writer. The dying words here quoted are inscribed on his monument in Trinity Churchyard, Broadway, New York.

Lieutenant Ludlow, of the *Chesapeake*, who was lying severely wounded on the *Shannon*, and doomed in a few days to die, won the esteem of the British by rebuking one of his brother-officers who wished to throw an erroneous gloss over the capture. " Let me hear," said he, " no more of it while we are aboard this ship. We were fairly beaten." The stone which has been raised to the memory of Lawrence is also inscribed to the memory of this his favourite lieutenant.

James Bulger, one of the seamen of the *Shannon*, boarded without arms, or rather unarmed. His excuse was, " I knew I should find plenty lying about her decks." He afterwards picked up a boarding pike, with which he seems, from his own account, to have set to work in great earnest.

When, as previously related, Midshipman Smith of the *Shannon* boarded the *Chesapeake* off the foreyard of the *Shannon*, the last of the Americans who fled down the topmast backstay to the deck was one of the midshipmen of the *Chesapeake*. He was followed so closely by Smith that the latter alighted upon him and tumbled him over on the deck, at which he was so alarmed that he begged to have his life spared. Captain Broke, who was then being led, very seriously wounded, close by the spot, took the middy with him by the collar, and so saved his life.

The result of the action had been prophesied in the *Naval Chronicle*, some months previously, in the following lines :—

> " And as the war they did provoke,
>   We'll pay them with our cannon :
> The first to do it will be Broke,
>   In the gallant ship the *Shannon*."

Many BRITISH subjects were found on board the *Chesapeake*, who had helped to resist the boarders from the *Shannon* ; indeed, the men who attacked and wounded Captain Broke were British subjects. Some were traitors, and these, no doubt, fought desperately even against their own countrymen, knowing that, if captured, they could not expect a better fate than death. Wallis says : " My recollection of the traitors found on board the *Chesapeake* is simply this—that there were five, one of whom was subsequently executed, and the other four sentenced to be flogged round the fleet ; but I do not remember names. There were also many of her crew who had belonged to our navy, receiving their discharge when the war commenced, upon claiming American citizenship. Amongst the wounded were some of these, who surprised Dr. Rowlands,* when dressing their wounds, by asking him if he did not remember them as former shipmates."

The *Shannon* was, it is believed, steered into action by James Coull, who had been present at the battle of Trafalgar, and who was now a petty officer and volunteer. He received in the wrist a ball which traversed his arm, but stuck to his post, and afterwards formed one of the boarding party, receiving a wound in the head while scrambling on board. His arm was subsequently amputated, but for many years he continued to go to sea, and ultimately died on October 1st, 1880, in the ninety-fifth year of his age. He was buried at Montrose, and, as an instance of the pride which is still felt in the famous achievement of the *Shannon*, it may be mentioned that his remains were interred with full military honours by detachments from both branches of the service, the coffin being borne by the coast-guard and a farewell volley fired. As an additional mark of respect, the shipping in the harbour exhibited colours at half-mast. There are many who will remember the portrait of his weather-beaten

---

* Surgeon at the Naval Hospital at Halifax.

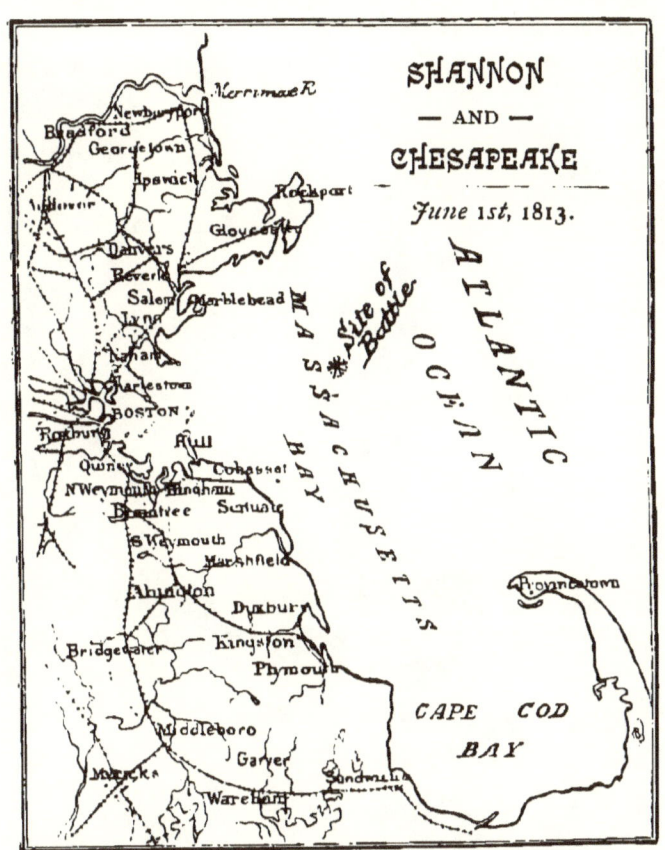

THE SITE OF THE BATTLE WAS MARKED ON THIS CHART BY
SIR PROVO WALLIS.

countenance which was exhibited last year at the Royal Naval Exhibition.

A great deal of controversy has taken place over a period of many years, between English and American writers, as to the relative strengths of the *Shannon* and the *Chesapeake*. By clever manipulation of figures as to displacement, weight, nature and destructive power of projectiles—by giving prominence to those points which seem to be in their favour and rendering obscure those which would tell against them, and in other ways, Americans have tried, not unnaturally perhaps, to minimise the brilliancy of the success which the *Shannon* obtained. The discussion seems unlikely to end, for quite recently there appeared in an American magazine an article attempting to disparage the *Shannon's* victory, and soon after, in another number of the same magazine, a criticism from one of her supporters. After the lapse of so many years it is, of course, impossible to suppose that those who renew these discussions are actuated by any feeling of hostility or resentment, which must have died long since. We still glory in the *Shannon's* achievement, and no one perhaps knows better than Sir Provo Wallis how American naval men can themselves talk with admiration of the good old English ship and her officers.

The Americans of Boston itself sumptuously entertained Sir Provo, as an officer of the *Shannon*, when in later years he was commanding the *Niemen* on the North American coast, and subsequently, on his visiting Boston again in 1846, and when, it is believed for the first time, " Yankee doodle " and " God save the Queen " were played one immediately after the other. Sir Provo in the same friendly spirit had long before said : " Lawrence displayed great skill and tactics when closing with us to prevent our fire, which, however, we did not attempt, for Broke had given orders not to fire whilst the gallant fellow kept his head towards us," and there can be no doubt that the gallantry of this noble man, which had earned for him the name of " the American Nelson," has ever been admired by our own countrymen.

I shall not attempt here to maintain any position that may appear to have been weakened by attack in the discussions to which I have referred, but leave those who are sufficiently interested to investigate the circumstances for themselves, merely remarking that, as there are many works dealing with the subject in both countries, a good deal of time will be occupied in the task. It will, however, not be out of place for me to say that, so far as my investigations have carried me, and they have been fairly exhaustive, no doubt is left on my mind that even though Broke, by his capable management, had undoubtedly got his men into a very high state of efficiency, the vessels

were not quite equally matched, and that such
advantage as there was rested with the *Chesapeake,*
possessing as she did a much greater number of
men, and being of at least equal power and better
fitted for the action : iudeed, had it not been so, it
is difficult to understand why the Americans should
have been so confident of her success. That they
were even jubilant over the prospect of victory for
their vessel is clearly shown by what appears in
this volume, and by the following extract from remarks made by Mr. Rush, the United States Minister
himself. He says :—

"The *Chesapeake*, it is true, was captured. The
English captain won his prize gallantly; let no
American gainsay this. We heard how the achievement was hailed in England, the more as it had
been preceded by a series of encounters terminating
differently. But with whatever satisfaction received
there, I cannot think it equalled the opposite feeling
in the United States. I remember (what American
does not?) the first rumour of it. I remember the
startling sensation. I remember at first the universal incredulity. I remember how the post-offices
were thronged for successive days with anxious thousands ; how collections of citizens rode out for
miles on the highway, accosting the mail to catch
something by anticipation. At last, when the
certainty was known, I remember the public gloom."

The action, it is perhaps needless to say, was in

both countries made the subject of many poems and rhymes, most of which were more remarkable for the bitter feeling they expressed than for their elevated tone.   There is not sufficient space here to set any of them out at length, but I will extract a few verses from a poem by a naval officer, Lieutenant M. Montague, R.N., after I have inserted a rather smart impromptu, which was written as soon as it was known that the Bostonians had made preparations to entertain the victors and vanquished at dinner :—

IMPROMPTU.

" The bold *Chesapeake*
　Came out on a freak,
And swore she'd soon silence our cannon ;
　While the Yankees in port
　Stood to laugh at the sport,
And see her tow in the brave *Shannon.*

　Quite sure of the game,
　As from harbour they came,
A dinner and wine they bespoke :
　But for *meat* they got *balls*
　From our staunch wooden walls,
And the dinner engagement was—BROKE."

EXTRACT FROM LIEUTENANT MONTAGUE'S POEM.

" The hero heard the joyful sounds
As, bleeding fast with ghastly wounds,
　All faint and pale he fell ;
And as his sailors bare him down,
' Cheer up !' said he, ' the day's your own,
　My wounds will soon be well.'

Exhausted nature would no more—
Let balmy rest the chief restore,
　And soothe his anguish'd pain :

Meanwhile brave Wallis may supply
His Captain's place and Falkiner vie
   In skill, nor vie in vain.

Go then, Columbia ! boast no more,
But weep your short liv'd triumphs o'er ;
   Your *Chesapeake* is lost !
This day our British tars have shown,
With skill and valour all their own,
   How poor, how false your boast."

This justly celebrated action, which has been truthfully described as one rarely equalled and never surpassed, undoubtedly had a far-reaching effect, and might indeed be said to have virtually put an end to that unhappy war, which fortunately has not yet been, and which every one must hope never will be, renewed.

The news of the victory was received in England at the same time as that of Wellington's success at Vittoria, and there was of course great rejoicing over the double event, one of the toasts being " An *English* Broke and an *Irish* river."

It would, perhaps, be wearying to prolong this account of the most important conflict in which Wallis was ever engaged, so much having already been written upon it by various historians; and having now placed before the reader those particulars of it which I have thought would be most interesting, I will turn my attention a little more closely to our hero himself, who, while having so many of his companions cut down by his side, had come out of the conflict without injury.

6

i

V.

THE VOYAGE TO HALIFAX AND RECEPTION THERE.

CHAPTER V.

THE VOYAGE TO HALIFAX AND RECEPTION THERE

IT was after the battle was over that the trial of Wallis commenced. His brave captain having been struck down and the first lieutenant killed, Wallis was left in control of two ships, crowded with dead and wounded, upon an enemy's coast, with formidable hostile cruisers probably not far distant, and with prisoners who would be but too glad of the opportunity of avenging the deaths of their comrades; added to which were the dangers of navigating what has been described as the most dangerous part of the American coast.

Wallis was young to undertake the serious responsibility which thus devolved upon him—of keeping in safety the *Shannon* and her prize during a voyage of some days until the harbour at Halifax should be reached. He was then but twenty-two years of age, and the risks involved in his task were such as might well have caused an older and more experienced man no little anxiety. He fully felt the burden which rested upon him, and proved himself worthy of his position. He says that during the whole voyage, which lasted nearly six days, he scarcely slept, and never once changed or removed his clothes, so deeply concerned was he regarding the safety of the vessels, until they arrived at their destination. His efforts were ably supported by Lieutenant Falkiner, to whose charge he had entrusted the *Chesapeake* immediately after the conclusion of the action, and on the 6th of June, 1813, both ships were safely brought to anchor in Halifax harbour.

It has often occurred to me, that of all the striking scenes of which the great ocean has been the voiceless witness, this short voyage of five days and nights must have been one of the most impressive to the contemplative mind. The *Shannon* and *Chesapeake* were within signalling distance of each other. From on board the victorious but silent *Shannon*, the dead Watt, Aldham, Dunn, and their comrades, had been consigned to the great deep. All hands were earnestly employed in repairing damages and exchanging prisoners, but not a voice above the ordinary tone was heard, for the gallant Broke lay in his own cabin, on the verge of insensibility from loss of blood, and the order "Silence fore and aft" had been issued

LIEUTENANT PROVO WALLIS

AT THE TIME OF HIS VICTORIOUS ENTRY INTO HALIFAX HARBOUR.

at the suggestion of Dr. Jack. On the *Chesapeake*
her former captain, but yesterday a tower of strength
and in the prime of manhood, was dying of wounds
inflicted by those who now exerted themselves to the
utmost to save him from their effect. In silent procession, with such solemnity on board, the good ships
travelled on their errand of mercy to the wounded,
and with the glorious news of victory for the millions
who would rejoice to receive it.

During the voyage the brave Lawrence died of his
wounds, and Wallis was once alarmed by the approach
of ships, which fortunately proved to be friends,
though at first believed to be enemies. It has been
related, too, that the prisoners on board the *Chesapeake* planned a rising to recapture that ship. It
is said that one evening the gunner was observed
supplying the officers' cabins with arms and ammuni-
tion. "Why," exclaimed ——, "you do not suppose
we could think of rising after you have treated us so
kindly ? " " You may rise as soon as you please ; you
see we are ready for you," was the blunt reply.

Commander Raymond, who, on the *Shannon*, was
one of the combatants in the action, and was on
board the *Chesapeake* during her voyage to Halifax,
confirms the story of this intended rising in a letter
written to me some years since ; but Admiral Wallis
states, in one of his communications, that if such
an attempt was made it was never reported to him
by Lieutenant Falkiner.

The voyage was not otherwise eventful, but the following account of it will be interesting because coming from Admiral Wallis himself. He says :—

" After finding that my captain was *hors de combat* and the first lieutenant killed, my first care was to get the prisoners secured, which was an easy matter, as the *Chesapeake* had upon deck some hundreds of handcuffs in readiness for us. So we ornamented them with their own manacles.

" Having at 10 p.m. knotted the rigging, fished the masts, and cleaned up our decks, we made sail and ran off shore until daylight of the 2nd, and then hove to, to complete our necessary repairs, after which we shaped a course for Halifax. On our way thither we fell in with the *Sceptre*, seventy-four, and *Loire* frigate. The weather at the time was thick, and until we exchanged numbers I was not a little alarmed, thinking they might be the *President* and *Congress*, who were cruising, it was said, in our track. Having ascertained who they were, I telegraphed,—' We have many wounded; do not detain us, as I am anxious to get them into hospital.'

" Nothing else occurred worth notice until we reached Sambro' lighthouse, off the harbour of Halifax, on the 4th June, when Captain Lawrence of the *Chesapeake* died of his wounds. Unfortunately, a dense fog kept us out until Sunday, the 6th, but on the morning of that day the fog lifted a little and we got a glimpse of the harbour's mouth, and in the afternoon reached our anchorage. As we passed the wharves, the whole population seemed to have turned out to welcome us with hearty cheers; and ships in port received us with yards manned, bands playing, etc. With regard to the occurrences on shore, Judge Haliburton's account will be better than anything I could tell you. Immediately we had anchored the wounded were sent to the hospital, and Captain Broke to the Commissioner's house in the dockyard, where he remained until the *Shannon* was ordered for England. Shortly after our arrival the first lieutenant of the *Chesapeake* (Ludlow) died of his wounds. Both Lawrence and he were buried at Halifax with military honours; but, shortly afterwards, the American Government sent a cartel to Halifax asking for their remains. The request met with a ready compliance, and they were taken to the United States, where they were reinterred with great pomp."

Sir Provo adds—"On the day following our action, Captain Lawrence expressed a wish to see our surgeon, who was immediately sent to him, and his report was that he found Lawrence mortally wounded. All that passed between them was—'Doctor, what is your opinion of my wounds?' Mr. Jack (our surgeon) replied, 'Sir, I grieve to tell you that I cannot entertain a hope of your recovery.' Lawrence was perfectly composed, but made no reply, and died on June 4th, the day we sighted Sambro' lighthouse.

Ludlow did not die for a week or more subsequently at the Naval Hospital. Ludlow's death was unexpected, for he had been making rapid progress towards recovery, but a sudden change in his head-wound carried him off. He was a very noble-minded man, and I have a vivid recollection of a conversation I had with him one day whilst sitting by his bedside (which was my daily custom after his wounds had been dressed), at the close of which he remarked, ' Well, I must say it was a gloriously fair stand-up fight. I fully expected a different result: the day, however, contrary to expectation, was nobly won by yourselves, and now behold how different is our lot; nevertheless, I hope to live, and should like to try it again.' "

The condition of Captain Broke upon the arrival of the ships at Halifax was most critical. Part of his skull had been hewn away, and the brain remained open to view. His friend, Commissioner Wodehouse, came on board, and having seen him returned to the deck, and leaning on the *Shannon's* capstan avowed, with a generous burst of sorrow, his belief that Broke could never recover. Said Wallis, " Leave it to me ; have his room ready in an hour, and I'll answer for his being there." Wodehouse, inspired by this confidence, departed on his errand. "Now, Sir," said Wallis to his almost exhausted commander, "I want you freed from all this noise and disturbance. I have had everything prepared, and I want to take you on shore." "Do with me as you please," was the gentle answer of the brave man ; and immediately the lashings of the cot were severed, and the *Shannons* chosen for the honoured task tenderly bore their commander on deck, and then as gently lowered him over the side into the boat his young lieutenant had carefully prepared for his reception.

Among the many touching incidents which attended the gallant *Shannon's* victorious return to Halifax, was predominantly the reception of Wallis by his family and the friends who had known him from boyhood, and who were now proud of him indeed.

In the crowd of strangers and friends which, on that Sunday evening of the *Shannon's* entry, hurried down to the King's Wharf to meet the victors on their arrival, was Wallis's townsman and friend, Thomas C. Haliburton, who was not then more than seventeen years of age. Many years afterwards, when he had passed his seventieth year, and but one year before his death, we were on a visit together in Suffolk, as the guests of the late Admiral Sir George Broke-Middleton, the then sole surviving son of the captain of the *Shannon*, and visited Broke Hall, Nacton, where the figure-head of the *Shannon*, a colossal female bust, ornamented with a necklace of gilded roundlets, had found a resting-place. I well remember the deep emotion with which this eminent man regarded the relic. "Fifty years ago I pulled beneath it in my boat, a boy of seventeen, and now——." The sentence remained unfinished by him, but was not the less understood by the bystanders. Many and most interesting were his reminiscences of the Anglo-American war, and at the request of our host he recorded the impressions made on him by the arrival of the *Shannon* in a letter, which is that referred to by Sir Provo in his account of the journey to Halifax just given. Judge Haliburton's letter is as follows :—

"GORDON HOUSE, ISLEWORTH, *June 1st,* 1864.

"MY DEAR SIR GEORGE,—

"I have received your note requesting me to state my reminiscences of the arrival at Halifax (Nova Scotia) of H.M.S. the *Shannon,* with her prize the *Chesapeake.* I have much pleasure in complying with your wishes ; but, more than fifty years having elapsed since that event, I can now only recall to my mind some few of the leading incidents that at that time impressed themselves on my youthful imagination.

"The action was fought on the 1st June, 1813, and on the Sunday following the ships reached the harbour of Halifax. I was attending divine service in St. Paul's Church at that time, when a person was seen to enter hurriedly, whisper something to a friend in the garrison pew, and as hastily withdraw. The

effect was electrical, for, whatever the news was, it
flew from pew to pew, and one by one the congrega-
tion left the church. My own impression was that
there was a fire in the immediate vicinity of St.
Paul's; and the movement soon became so general
that I, too, left the building to inquire into the cause
of the commotion. I was informed by a person in
the crowd that 'an English man-of-war was coming
up the harbour with an American frigate as her
prize.' By that time the ships were in full view, near
George's Island, and slowly moving through the
water. Every housetop and every wharf was crowded
with groups of excited people, and, as the ships
successively passed, they were greeted with vociferous
cheers. Halifax was never in such a state of excite-
ment before or since. It had witnessed in former
days the departure of General Wolfe for an attack
on Louisburg, with a fleet of 140 sail, and also his
triumphant return. In later years the people had
assisted in fitting out the expedition, under Sir
George Prevost, for the capture of Martinique and
Guadaloupe; but nothing had ever excited the Hali-
gonians like the arrival of these frigates. It was no
new thing to see a British man-of-war enter the port
with a prize of equal or greater size than herself;
they regarded success as a matter of course. When,
therefore, the news came, some time previously, of
the capture of the *Guerriere* by the *Constitution*,
men were unwilling to believe it, considering such

an event as simply impossible. I can well remember
the gloom that hung over the community when the
official account was received. In common with all
others, old and young, although I participated in the
general sorrow that event occasioned, I was not surprised; for, though unable myself to judge of the
cause of the defeat, I had heard an experienced old
friend of mine (the Hon. S. B. Robie) foretell the
occurrence of disasters when our frigates should encounter those of the United States. He said the
latter had the scantling of seventy-fours, and were
equal to sixty-gun ships; that they were built with
remarkable strength, mounted heavier and more guns
than our ships of the same nominal rate, and were
commanded by very experienced officers. He added
that the American Government, by suddenly placing
an embargo on all the shipping in their ports, had the
seamen of the whole mercantile marine of their country at their disposal, and were thus enabled to man
their little navy with crews of picked men; while the
system they had adopted of seducing, by means of
extravagant bounties, the most skilled gunners to
desert from our ships, supplied their men-of-war with
a class of able-bodied and disciplined seamen who
would fight like demons, as the gallows awaited them
if taken prisoners.

" In addition to all these disadvantages, our naval
officers, he said, held their enemies too cheap, and
would some day be awakened to a knowledge of their

H.M.S. "SHANNON"

LEADING HER PRIZE, THE AMERICAN FRIGATE "CHESAPEAKE," INTO
HALIFAX HARBOUR, ON THE 6TH JUNE, 1813.

fatal mistake. The people of Halifax were under the same delusion as the navy, and equally ill-informed and rashly confident. The encounter of the *Guerriere* with the *Constitution* fully justified these forebodings of my friend. The relative strength of those ships was first made known after the action, the former mounting (if my memory serves me) only forty-nine guns, with a complement of 263 men, while the latter carried sixty guns, and had a crew of 450 men. The action was fought with great gallantry on our part, but with a want of discretion that, notwithstanding this great disparity, was said to have occasioned the loss of the ship. Other actions soon followed with the same inequality, and with a similar fatal result. It was, therefore, no wonder that the people of Halifax were so elated by what they considered a turn in the tide of luck, for it is now known that the action of the *Shannon* and the *Chesapeake* was the commencement of a series of signal victories. It proved the absolute necessity of filling up the crews of our fleet to their full complement, of introducing a stricter discipline, and maintaining a greater state of efficiency.

"It soon became known in Halifax that the ships now approaching were the *Shannon* and the *Chesapeake*, and that the former was in charge of Lieutenant Provo Wallis, a native of Halifax, who was in temporary command in consequence of the severe and dangerous wounds of her gallant captain.

This circumstance naturally added to the enthusiasm of the citizens, for they felt that through him they had some share in the honour of the achievement. No one could have supposed that these ships had been so recently engaged in mortal combat, for, as they slowly passed up to the dockyard, they appeared as if they had just returned from a cruise, their rigging being all standing and wholly uninjured. They were tolerably well matched in size, the *Chesapeake* being only seventy tons larger than her antagonist, and her broadside only fifty pounds heavier. The greatest disparity was in their respective crews, the American force outnumbering the British by 110 men—a superiority which would probably have proved fatal in a contest finally decided by boarding, had not her losses in killed and wounded reduced them to a nearer equality. Nor was the American commander (Lawrence) inferior to his opponent in courage and weight of character. He had, a short time previously, while in command of the U.S. sloop-of-war *Hornet*, captured, after a short and gallant contest, the sloop-of-war *Peacock*, one of the first ships of her class in the British navy. The *prestige* of his name was such that the inhabitants of Boston regarded the capture of the Britisher, who had so presumptuously challenged the *Chesapeake*, as a matter of positive certainty. Lawrence was especially popular with the American seamen, who, when they heard he had received the command

of the *Chesapeake*, flocked to his standard in great
numbers from all the adjacent ports, and enabled
him not only to fill up the full complement of the
ship's crew with picked men, but to add to their
number many additional volunteers selected from the
best seamen in the eastern states. No ship ever left
an American port so fully and ably manned as this
frigate. So entirely did the people of Boston anticipate an easy and a speedy victory, that they prepared
a banquet for the captors on their return from the
conflict, to which they magnanimously resolved to
invite Captain Broke and his officers. The wharf
from which the last boat was despatched to the ship
was crowded with an excited and exulting throng,
who cheered their departing countrymen. The feeling of confident triumph was, with one exception,
unanimous. A negro in the crowd, who had spent
the greater part of his life about the dockyard of
Halifax, observing in the boat a coloured friend, gave
vent to his humour or patriotism by saying, ' Good-
bye, Sam ; you is going to Halifax before you comes
back to Bosting ; give my lub to requiring friends,
and tell 'em I is berry well.' For this harmless but
inappropriate sally he was instantly thrown into the
dock, amid the execrations and derision of the enraged citizens, and narrowly escaped with his life.

"Of the action it would be presumption in me
to speak. You are in possession of official documents and authentic details, while all I know about

7

it is what I heard after the arrival of the belligerents in the harbour. In fifteen minutes after the first broadside was fired both ships were under weigh for Halifax, the *Shannon* leading the way and her prize following. The Bay of Boston at the time was filled with schooners, sloops, and sail-boats, to witness the combat; and the adjoining headlands, between the scene of action and Cape Cod, were crowded with people striving to catch a glimpse of the capture of the British frigate. When it was observed that she was in advance, and the *Chesapeake* following, it was unanimously agreed that she was endeavouring to escape, and that the latter was in full chase. The event was hailed with every noisy demonstration of joy, and was communicated to the city, where the only fear entertained was that she would not overtake her flying foe in time for the victorious officers to partake of the splendid banquet which had been provided for them. It was the last view the Bostonians were ever destined to have of their frigate, which had fulfilled the prophecy of the negro, and gone to visit Halifax.

" As soon as possible after the vessels had anchored near the dockyard there, a young friend and myself procured a boat and pushed off, to endeavour to obtain permission to visit them. We were refused admission to the *Shannon,* in consequence of Captain Broke requiring quiet and repose on account of his severe wounds, but were more fortunate in obtaining

access to the *Chesapeake.* Externally she looked,
as I have already said, as if just returned from a
short cruise; but internally the scene was one never
to be forgotten by a landsman. The deck had not
been cleaned (for reasons of necessity that were
obvious enough), and the coils and folds of ropes
were steeped in gore as if in a slaughter-house.
She was a fir-built ship, and her splinters had
wounded nearly as many men as the *Shannon's* shot.
Pieces of skin, with pendant hair, were adhering to
the sides of the ship; and in one place I noticed
portions of fingers protruding, as if thrust through
the outer wall of the frigate; while several of the
sailors, to whom liquor had evidently been handed
through the portholes by visitors in boats, were lying
asleep on the bloody floor as if they had fallen in
action and had expired where they lay. Altogether
it was a scene of devastation as difficult to forget
as to describe. It is one of the most painful
reminiscences of my youth, for I was but seventeen
years of age, and it made upon me a mournful
impression that, even now, after a lapse of half
a century, remains as vivid as ever.

"The guns of the *Chesapeake* had all names given
to them, which were painted in large white letters,
such as 'Free Trade,' 'Sailors' Rights,' 'Bloody
Murder,' 'Sudden Death,' 'Nancy Dawson,' etc. In
looking back on these arrangements, one cannot
help regarding with a feeling of contempt this

incessant and vulgar appeal to popular prejudice, now so common among the Americans. The two first mottoes, 'Free Trade' and 'Sailors' Rights,' are those which the Yankees have the least pretence of any civilised community on earth to claim to respect or protect. In trade they are close protectionists, and ever have been; and as for 'Sailors' Rights,' it is well known that there is more tyranny, oppression, and cruelty practised towards seamen in their navy and mercantile marine than in that of all other nations of the world combined. I observed on the quarterdeck the figure of a large man wrapped up in the American flag. I was told it was the corpse of the gallant Captain Lawrence, who fell in the discharge of his duty, and whose last words are reported to have been, 'Don't give up the ship.' He was buried at Halifax with all the respect due to his bravery and his misfortune.

"With the subsequent history of the *Chesapeake*, you are better acquainted than myself. She remained a long time in the harbour of Halifax, and finally proceeded to England, where she was broken up.

"The annals of the British navy furnish numerous instances of gallant frigate actions, but that of the *Shannon* and *Chesapeake* is equalled by few, and surpassed by none, while its consequences and effects on the subsequent events of the war render it, in my opinion, the most important one on record.

"The name of Broke will ever be regarded with

pride and pleasure by that service of which he was so distinguished a member ; and it must be a great gratification to his family and friends to know that that feeling is fully participated in by a grateful country.

"I am, my dear Sir George,

"Yours always,

"THOMAS C. HALIBURTON."

The following tribute paid to the British, by that charming and well-known American writer, Washington Irving, in his biography of Captain Lawrence, which was written shortly after Lawrence's death, is well worth repetition here, and will perhaps make a fitting close to this chapter. He says :—

"With feelings that swell our hearts, do we notice the honours paid to the brave Lawrence, at Halifax. When the ships arrived in port, a generous concern was expressed for his fate. The recollection of his humanity towards the crew of the *Peacock* was still fresh in every mind. His obsequies were celebrated with appropriate ceremonials, and an affecting solemnity. His pall was supported by the oldest captains in the British service that were in Halifax ; and the naval officers crowded to yield the last sad honours to a man who was late their foe, but now their foe no longer. There is a sympathy between gallant souls that knows no distinction of clime or nation. They honour in each other what they feel proud of in themselves. The group that gathered round the grave of Lawrence presented a scene worthy of the heroic days of chivalry. It was a complete triumph of the nobler feelings over the savage passions of war. We know not where most to bestow our admiration,—on the living, who showed such generous sensibility to departed virtue, or on the dead, in being worthy of such obsequies from such spirits. It is by deeds like these that we really feel ourselves subdued. The conflict of arms is ferocious, and triumph does but engender more deadly hostility ; but the contest of magnanimity calls forth the better feelings, and the conquest is over the affections. We hope that in such a contest we may never be outdone ; but that the present unhappy war may be continually softened and adorned by similar acts of courtesy and kindness on either part, thus sowing among present hostilities the quickening seeds of future friendship."

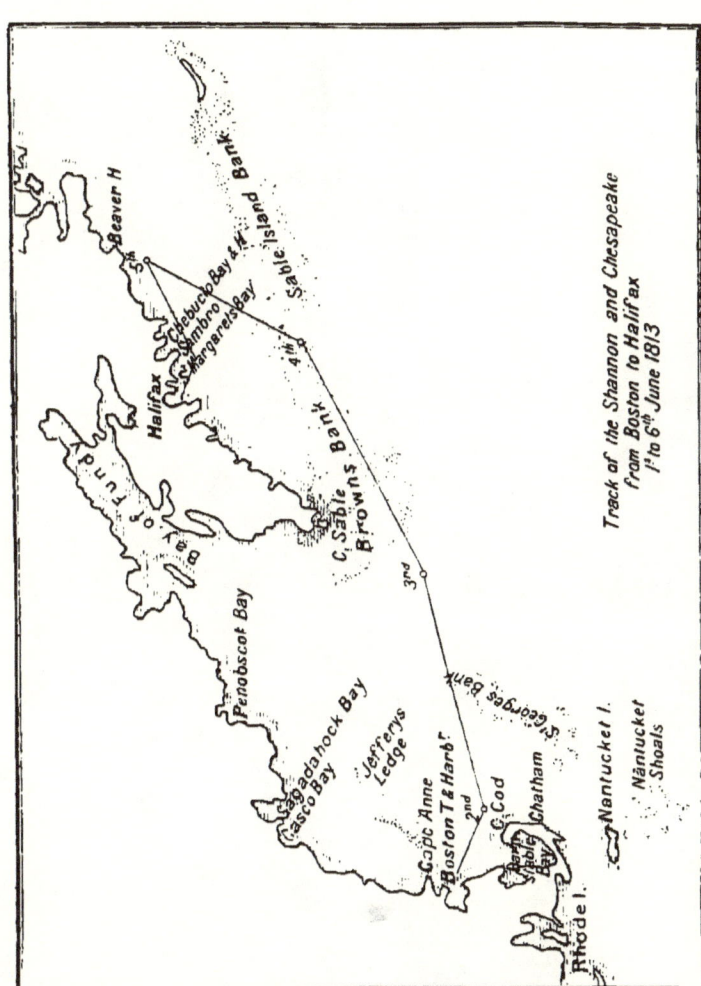

Track of the Shannon and Chesapeake
from Boston to Halifax
1st to 6th June 1813

THE TRACK WAS MARKED ON THIS CHART BY SIR PROVO WALLIS.

VI.

AT HALIFAX—THE OFFICIAL REPORT OF THE ACTION OF THE "SHANNON" AND "CHESAPEAKE"—PROMOTION, AND RETURN TO ENGLAND.

CHAPTER VI.

AT HALIFAX—THE OFFICIAL REPORT OF THE ACTION OF THE "SHANNON" AND "CHESAPEAKE"—PRO-MOTION, AND RETURN TO ENGLAND.

ON the morning following the arrival of the *Shannon* at Halifax, the senior officer in port, Captain the Hon. Bladen Capel, considering it desirable that the report of the *Shannon's* engagement with the *Chesapeake* should be forwarded to England as soon as possible, requested Wallis, as being now the senior officer in charge, to furnish an official account of the action. Wallis hesitated, however, to undertake this gratifying duty, because he was anxious Broke should tell his own story. He says: "I could not persuade myself to do this whilst there was a chance of my dear captain's strength enabling him to write with his own hand." He therefore informed Captain Capel that he would be obliged to him if he would wait a few days, and see whether Captain Broke might not be able to dictate a letter. Capel replied, "Very well, sir." Two days later Wallis was informed by Capel that he should send the *Nova Scotia* brig, commanded by Lieutenant Bartholomew Kent, to England on the 12th, and grant Lieutenant Falkiner permission to take charge of the letter which he expected Captain Broke would be enabled to dictate. No further communication took place between Capel and Wallis, and on the date last mentioned the *Nova Scotia* sailed without Wallis having seen the official letter which was taken in her, and which bore Captain Broke's name as the writer of it.

The official letter appears to have contained several inaccuracies, and having regard to his chief's state of health and the circumstances in which the letter had been sent, Wallis for a long time was firmly convinced that it was a concoction of Capel and others. He felt that he had been slighted by Capel, and in after years took a great deal of trouble to ascertain what was the true state of things in relation to the letter, and corresponded with Capel himself on the subject, when, as will be seen from the subjoined letter, the latter admitted that Broke was not in a fit state, for several days after his arrival at Halifax, to give an account of the action. Wallis also obtained from Dr. Rowlands, the surgeon who attended Broke, the certificate of which a copy is appended, and which confirmed Wallis's impressions.

LETTER FROM CAPTAIN CAPEL TO ADMIRAL WALLIS.

"*June* 19*th*, 1834.

" DEAR SIR,—

"I really do not quite understand what it is that you require of me to state (as far as my recollection may serve me) relative to the action between the *Shannon* and *Chesapeake*. In your letter of the 13th inst. you say: 'All I can ask of you is a statement that Sir P. Broke was not in a state (for several days) to give me an account of the action.' I can, of course, have no hesitation in stating that such was the fact; but surely you cannot expect that, after a lapse of twenty years, I can recollect what conversations may have passed between you and myself on that occasion. I, therefore, cannot answer any of the queries contained in your letter, which, indeed, becomes unnecessary, as I have stated all you require me to do, viz., that Sir P. Broke was not in a state (for several days) after his arrival at Halifax to give me an account of the action.

"I am, very truly yours,

"BLADEN CAPEL."

CERTIFICATE BY DR. ROWLANDS.

"These are to certify that I, the under-signed, David Rowlands, M.D., F.R.S., late Surgeon of H.M. Naval Hospital at Halifax, in Nova Scotia, was there when H.M.S. *Shannon* arrived with her prize the American frigate *Chesapeake*, on Sunday, June 6th, 1813; the former was commanded by the present Captain Wallis, owing to the dreadful wound which Captain Broke had received in the action with the enemy a few days previous. On June 7th I was requested by Mr. Alexander Jack, the surgeon of the *Shannon*, to visit Captain Broke, confined to bed at the Commissioner's house in the dockyard, and found him in a very weak state, with an extensive sabre wound on the side of the head, the brain exposed to view for three inches or more; he was unable to converse save in monosyllables, and I am sure totally unable to dictate or write an account of the action for some time afterwards, owing to his severe wounds, loss of blood, and the shock his whole frame must have experienced by the blow on the head.

"I continued to attend him twice a day for weeks afterwards, in conjunction with Mr. Jack, to whom every credit is justly due for his skilful treatment and care in bringing his brave captain on shore alive.

"I grant this certificate to Captain Wallis, being called upon to do so by the death of Mr. Jack, the surgeon.

"Given under my hand this 8th day of December, 1841.

"D. ROWLANDS, M.D."

It may be here remarked that although the official report is dated on the day of the *Shannon's* arrival at Halifax, it would appear from the conversation between Captain Capel and Wallis, which took place some days after, that it was not actually written on that day.

Admiral King, who possessed a directly personal knowledge of these occurrences, states that Broke was greatly annoyed by the injustice which had been done to Wallis, and by the inaccuracies which the official letter contained.

In the end Wallis had, at least, the satisfaction of ascertaining that the letter was not a concoction as he had at first supposed, but had, in fact, been sanctioned by Broke, although it seems clear that he was not in a fit state to correct a long letter with regard to its details. The letter was, in all probability, to a great extent prepared from reports made by some of his officers; and, indeed, Broke himself appears to have stated that some of the errors could be traced to officers who, for his amusement while he was lying ill, had told him stories which were embodied in the letter, although it was doubtless not intended they should find a place there by those who told them. It would also appear that other errors arose from imperfect commitment to paper of the facts as then related. Admiral Wallis has since, in one of his letters to me, stated that it is not his wish that any strictures should be noted against the errors in the official letter, as they are now fully accounted for; but whether he ever forgot the manner in which he was treated, in not being consulted as to the contents of the letter, or selected to carry it to England, is a question which cannot be answered.

It may be well to shortly state what the inaccuracies in the official letter were, as explained by Admiral Wallis, as it will then be seen that while they were sufficient to throw doubt on the authenticity of the letter, they were not of the first importance, and the letter was, in fact, abundantly correct on graver matters.

The official report of Captain Broke says: "After exchanging two or three broadsides, the enemy's ship fell on board of us, her mizen-channels locking in with our fore-rigging. I went forward to ascertain her position, and, observing that the enemy were flinching from their guns, I gave orders to prepare for boarding. Our gallant band appointed for that purpose immediately rushed in under their respective officers."

The description by Admiral Wallis is as follows:—
" The cannonading continued for only eleven minutes, when the *Chesapeake,* who had got before our beam, was taken aback, and, making a stern board, dropped into us just abaft our fore-channels. Broke, who saw the confusion on board of her, ran forward, calling out, ' Follow me who can,' and jumped on board, supported by all who were within hearing. A minute had hardly elapsed before the ships had separated, and a general cry was then raised, ' Cease firing,' and by the time I had got upon the quarter-deck from the aftermost part of our maindeck, the ships had got so far asunder that it was *impossible* to throw any more men on board of her. I must here observe that *no orders were given to prepare to board,* but the happy moment was seized as already described."

The official letter goes on to say:—" Having received a severe sabre wound at the onset, while charging a party of the enemy who had rallied on their forecastle, I was only capable of giving command till assured our conquest was complete; and then, directing Second-Lieutenant Wallis to take charge of the *Shannon* and secure the prisoners, I left the Third Lieutenant, Mr. Falkiner (who had headed the maindeck boarders), in charge of the prize "; further, that " Lieutenants John and Law,

8

of the marines, boarded at the head of their respective divisions"; and that "Mr. Smith, who commanded in our foretop, stormed the enemy's foretop from the foreyard-arm, and destroyed all the Americans remaining in it"; and finally, that "both ships came out of action in the most beautiful order, their rigging appearing as perfect as if they had only been exchanging a salute."

Sir Provo says: "It was mere invention Smith's having stormed her foretop, but he did board her from our foreyard, and slid down one of her backstays. Neither did the officers of marines board, for when I took command I found them there. It was equally erroneous to say that the ships came out of action as perfect as if they had only been exchanging a salute, the fact being that our lower rigging was all cut through, and the masts consequently unsupported, so that had any sea been on they would have gone over the side. Finally, the story of Broke having given me the orders to take the charge of the *Shannon* and Falkiner the *Chesapeake* was fabulous."

The following is the recommendation of Wallis and Falkiner for promotion which is contained in the official report of the action:—

"I beg to recommend these officers most strongly to the Commander-in-chief's patronage for the gallantry they displayed during the action, and the skill and judgment with which they carried on the anxious duties which afterwards devolved upon them."

Notwithstanding this recommendation Falkiner was never promoted to the rank of captain, but took it by retirement. Wallis considered that the Admiralty treated Falkiner badly in this respect, and states that he was as gallant a fellow as ever lived, and conducted the *Chesapeake* into the harbour of Halifax highly to his satisfaction. Wallis was more fortunate, and his promotion to the rank of commander came quickly, although not before he had taken another cruise in the *Shannon* as a lieutenant. He says :—

" When the *Shannon* was refitted and ready for sea, the port admiral (afterwards Sir E. Griffiths Colpoys) sent for me, and after expressing his regret that he could not any longer permit me to continue in command of the *Shannon*, in accordance with the rules of the service, informed me that he had given Commander Senhouse, of the *Martin*, an acting order as captain for a short cruise, as Broke was too unwell to resume his duty. He was pleased to add that, although there was not a doubt of my promotion, still he did not officially know of it : he therefore hoped (and told me it was Broke's particular wish) that I should not have any objection to do the duty of first lieutenant, as I was perfectly aware of Broke's mode of government, and that Senhouse had promised to consult me. I did remain. We sailed, and for a short time resumed our old cruising ground off Boston. We detained two Spanish ships, which did not, however, prove to be prizes. Upon our return to Halifax my promotion, with a gratifying letter from the Admiralty, relative to my conduct in the action with the *Chesapeake*, was given to me, and Lieutenant Clark replaced me in the *Shannon*."

Besides the letter of thanks from the Admiralty Wallis received what he, perhaps, equally prized, viz., a sword and pair of epaulettes from his captain, accompanied by the following note :—

> "DEAR WALLIS,—
>
> "I send you a captain's sword, and hope you will soon have the opportunity of drawing it with success in the same cause which gave you the rank.
>
> "I am, etc."

What the noble Broke thought of Wallis, whom in after years he delighted to call "his dear shipmate," may be seen from the following testimonial, which was given to Wallis after he had received his promotion :—

> "This is to certify that Captain P. W. P. Wallis served a year and a half as lieutenant of Her Majesty's ship *Shannon* (then under my

command), and proved himself a most diligent, zealous, and confidential officer, and more particularly so in the action with the American frigate *Chesapeake* in June 1813, when, by his bravery and skilful management, he effected important service, having the command of both the *Shannon* and her prize on my being disabled by wounds.

" P. B. V. Broke,

" Late Captain of H.M.S. ' Shannon.'

"Signed at Broke Hall, *January 20th*, 1815."

During the time Captain Broke was recovering from his wounds sufficiently to enable him to leave Halifax, he received assiduous attention from Wallis's sister, then the wife of Lord James Townshend, who, it will have been seen, commanded the *Æolus*, one of the companion ships of the *Shannon* during some of her cruises after she was joined by Wallis. Captain Broke has described Lady Townshend as " an unaffected, though pretty girl, and of sweet disposition." At the time he received his wounds, Broke wore in his bosom what in writing to his wife he describes as her " little blue satin cover, with the cherished lock of hair." This cover was stained with the captain's blood, but the hair was preserved dry. Wallis had removed the locket from his captain's neck after the battle, and given it to his sister, Lady Townshend, to

be re-covered, and she, in making the new cover, imi-
tated the original exactly, much to Captain Broke's
satisfaction. The original was retained by Wallis
for some time, and ultimately given by him to his
captain's son, Admiral Sir George Broke-Middleton,
to whom I have already referred.

While lying ill at Halifax, Captain Broke received
the following letters from his excellent wife, Louisa,
daughter of Sir William Middleton, Bart., of Shrub-
land Park, Suffolk :—

LADY BROKE'S LETTERS TO HER HUSBAND ON THE CAPTURE OF THE " CHESAPEAKE," 1813.*

" SUNDAY.

". . . Yesterday, Lady Nelson, hearing that I
was here, kindly came over to see me, and made
many inquiries after you. She is not looking so
well as when I saw her at Dawlish. She is going
from Exmouth to Teignmouth for a month, so I fear
I shall not see her again. I wished her to stay and
drive with me ; but she could not, on account of
Captain Nisbett, who still lives with her, and to
whom she devotes her whole time.

" I must hasten to finish this, my love, as I find

---

* It was the wish and intention of Sir G. Broke-Middleton that
these letters should have found their proper place in the memoir of
his father ; but they were not recovered until some years after its
publication. They may suitably be inserted here. Many of the names
mentioned therein will be familiar to the reader of history.

there is a convoy collecting at Torbay for America; the *Talbot* is one of the ships now there, and I shall send this with some papers on board. The *Martin,* I see, is also at Falmouth for the same destination. How provoking that after all your care Rodgers with *Congress* should make their escape, also that *Chesapeake* should get safe in! Their usual good fortune attends them. *I trust it will be your turn next.* After copying your order to Child for Mr. B., I forwarded it to him, as you desired. I feel much obliged, but hope not to have occasion to draw upon him beyond my quarter during your absence; nothing but to pay my expenses to come out to you could induce me to do so, and that I would most readily do to-morrow were it not for the hope of seeing *you home.* I see the *Cumberland* and a large fleet have arrived from the Leeward Islands; but I fear I shall not get letters by her. I told your good mother all you told me respecting poor deserted Nacton; but you will have seen by my letters, long before you get this, that Sir R. and Lady Harland are now in it, while they are adding to Orwell. Indeed, I feel with you that I should not be inclined immediately on your return to begin afresh at Nacton : it will require too much thought and attention. Our dear children are all charmingly, and enjoy very much the hay-fields, which are just now in high beauty and fragrance; and I am sure my beloved Philip will be glad to hear that I frequently ride out on a very quiet

donkey, which is let out here, and which also carries
Mrs. Sutton. All my *little party* accompany me;
and with the aid of the servant, at hand to assist me
when I take fright, I do very well. The country
about here is extremely beautiful, with nice, shady
lanes, which are delightful,—the banks and hedges
on each side lined with roses and honeysuckle, which
the dear little ones delight in bringing in abundance
for Mama. Indeed, had I but my dear Philip here,
I could be very happy; but, *with him*, what place
would be otherwise? Mrs. Sutton took Phil and
me to church with her, and took a little airing after.
The weather is now beautiful. I hope you have
enjoyed some fine of late. I yesterday heard from
Sophy Dashwood: she is with her father and sisters
at Weymouth, and wants much to persuade me to
come and take a lodging near them. Our dear
children unite in kindest love and kisses to their dear
Papa: and Willy says, 'Tell him to come home.'
Dear fellow, he neither wants to be told or reminded
of what is so near his heart. May God speedily
place him in a situation to do so, without reproach!
May He bless and preserve you in all happiness, for
the sake of—

"Your ever affectionate and anxious

"Loo.

"P.S.—Pray continue to write as much and as
frequently as you can, my beloved husband. I enclose

you a little watchcase I have had made for you. All
the cottagers are lace-makers, but have not tempted
me into any great extravagance hitherto."

"BUDLEIGH SALTERTON, *July* 11*th*, 1813.

"This has been a day of great trial to me, my
beloved husband. I went to church with Phil and
Loo in the morning, and Admiral and Mrs. Sutton
accompanied me. The newspapers we took in the
carriage were filled with joy and exultation at your
success; and such praise bestowed in the House
by Mr. Croker and others on your gallant and noble
conduct as was almost too much for your Loo. It
was indeed most gratifying to me to hear you so
highly spoken and thought of by the *whole country.*
You will say it is enough to make me proud,—that I
ever was, and had reason to be, of you; but, my
beloved Philip, is it true that you *challenged the*
'*Chesapeake*'? for the papers of to-day mention that
as being the case, and, not having heard so from
yourself, I know not whether to give credit to it or
not. Your official letter is not yet printed, but I
hope to see that to-morrow. I sent a few lines to
you yesterday by good Mrs. Samwell, to Plymouth,
as she was obliged to return home; and I was anxious
you should know I had received your letters, my
love, to 12th June. And I am preparing this to send
by Captain Swaine, who is still in Torbay, collecting
convoy for Halifax; but long ere they reach that

port I trust *you* will be in England. *How anxious* I am of later accounts of you, to know that you are continuing to do well, your dear head healed, and your strength repaired, and you ordered home! What joy will that news give me! Yet how *long* will the time then appear till you arrive! but I will and must endeavour to be calm and patient, trusting in a merciful Providence for His further support and protection, ever grateful for His goodness in saving so valuable a life, when in the midst of so many and great dangers. I was happy in being able to-day to offer up in the house of God my humble and un-feigned thanks to Him for this greatest of goodness towards me. May I ever keep it in mind, and render me more worthy of His love and yours! Admiral Sutton heard to-day from Captain Hotham to 1st June; he was then well at Bermuda, with Sir J. Warren and his squadron, who were to sail from thence shortly for the American coast, carrying out with them three thousand troops, the *Diadem* and *Diomede* having joined them; but learnt no news. I sent many letters by Captain Hanchett to my Philip, but know not if he touched at Halifax in his way. I hope you will get letters enough from me to amuse you during your stay at Halifax. How I wish *myself there* to nurse and attend upon you; but it will be too late to venture out now. God bless you! I must go to rest: it is getting late.

" *Monday Evening.*—The fisherman has just called

to say he goes this evening to Torbay, so I must make haste and finish this for my beloved Philip. Must just tell him to-day's paper says that Lord Melville thought so highly of the action, or rather of yourself and the officers of the *Shannon*, that as a mark of it the two surviving lieutenants are to be promoted to commanders, and the two middies who boarded are to be the lieutenants of the *Shannon*, to replace the above. I cannot help hoping, and have little doubt, that Samwell is one. I shall rejoice if it proves so. My Philip will, I know, be happy to hear such are Lord Melville's intentions. I wish poor King had been with you. I fully expected to have heard from your dear mother to-day, but was disappointed; I got no letters. Our dear children are all well. Dear baby put into the sea this morning for the *first time*, and not the least alarmed. I trust it will strengthen him. How I long to show him to his father! and trust he will smile on him as he does on me. Dear Phil is only hoping you may be home before his holidays are over, which will be about the 28th of this month. I think, if not summoned to Plymouth before by *you*, to take him back to Ottery on the 31st. I intend going from thence on the 4th August, if Mrs. Samwell can get me a house in George's Street by that time; hers, I fear, will not be ready, as the Admiral has not yet left it. He is going to Buxton till Admiral Domett comes to succeed. Dear Loo has not recovered her good plight since the measles, but I hope soon will. Dear Willy is getting on charmingly, though you must expect still to see him but a little creature, possessed, thank God! with charming spirits. You will not, I hope, pass Plymouth without our seeing you; if you cannot stay there you must come and take us on board. Of poor Mrs. Aldham I have not heard, but hope to do so to-morrow through Mrs. Samwell. At this instant the poor little boys of this village are illuminating a little bridge opposite this house in honour of the glorious event. And I am illuminating too; but my mind would be much easier if I could hear again, and my beloved Philip was well. I must seal this up. Heaven bless and protect you, and conduct you safe into the arms of your ever affectionate—

"Loo.

"The dear children send kindest love and kisses."

"BUDLEIGH SALTERTON, *July* 18*th*, 1813.

"I have for the last week, my beloved Philip, received so many congratulations on your safety and success that I have been writing three or four letters every day, but literally have not had leisure to write to *you* since I sent my letters last Monday on board the *Talbot*, in Torbay, where I believe she *still* remains waiting for convoy; and I have now so little idea that my letters will reach you before you have left Halifax for England, that I am not so *earnest*

about it as I otherwise should be. Another week has
passed, no further accounts from *you*. *I cannot
express to you* how *very* anxious I am for my next
accounts of you, to be assured of your continued well-
doing, to know that your wounds *are* healed, and that
you have got your orders from Sir John Warren to
return home ; but I feel also convinced that you will
be equally anxious with *myself* to forward these
delightful tidings to me as soon as it is in your power
to do so. The horrible distance that we are separated
from each other is now less bearable than ever ; but
I *do* trust it will not be long before my mind is rendered more at ease on your account ; for, till I hear
again of your safety and well-doing, I cannot be
happy. The newspapers have, till the last two days,
been filled with encomiums on your most gallant
achievement and heroism, which has confessedly
never been surpassed in the annals of naval history,
if ever equalled. You will believe how interesting
and delightful they have been to me ; and, now that
they cease to dwell longer upon it, how very insipid
and uninteresting they appear to me ! On Tuesday
last I received from Mr. Croker a very handsome
letter of congratulation, and enclosing at the same
time a copy of your excellent letter, which does so
much credit to your head and heart, my Philip, that
those who have read it cannot help admiring the
relation. He adds that the Lords Commissioners, to
show the high sense they entertained of your gallant

and successful conduct, have ordered a medal for you, which *I* shall be proud to see you *wear*. The City of London has also voted you thanks, with the freedom of the City, and intend presenting you with a sword of one hundred guineas' value. All these honours are most gratifying ; but, after all, my Philip's own feelings must be his best and surest reward. I am sure you will be happy to hear that Lieutenants Wallis and Falkiner are to be promoted to commanders ; the two midshipmen who boarded (but whose names I cannot learn) are to be promoted to lieutenants on board the *Shannon*. This must be doubly gratifying to them, but I want much to know *who* they are. Poor Mrs. Aldham was greatly distressed, but I am happy to hear she is now rather better. Thinking it might afford her some consolation under her affliction to be informed what you had said in your letter respecting Mr. Aldham, I copied that part of it and sent her. The mention you there made of her was truly kind, and very like yourself. I have little doubt of your pleading *in vain*, for by your conduct, my love, you have secured to yourself such interest and *universal* love and admiration that you might ask for what *you please* without a fear of being denied. But this is my fourth letter to-day and it is getting late, so God bless and love you, as I do !

" 19*th*.—By this day's post I have another letter from my friend Mr. Croker, in answer to my inquiries respecting the probable return of the *Shannon* ; and he says, 'I am sorry I cannot give you any precise information as to the return of the *Shannon*. We have every reason to believe that she is on her way home; but it is not in consequence of orders from England, but on account of her having been so very long abroad.' This is very comforting; but I still want to know *more*, to be assured you are actually coming. But nothing has arrived since the *Nova Scotia*, to allow my getting letters. I have also got a most kind letter of congratulation from my dear brother, who is now staying with my Uncle and Aunt Acton at Tendring. He says it is whispered in London that you will either have a red riband or a baronetcy. It is also said that the West India merchants mean to make you some handsome present. He wishes with me that it may be a little cash to furnish Nacton with, as, when he dined the other day with the 'Harlands,' he said the poor house looked miserable, and in want of a few thousands to be expended upon it. He says you are not likely to receive more than £1200 for the capture of the frigate. I do not care for money so long as I get my beloved husband home safe and well,—that is my most earnest wish; and that, *once* there, we may be permitted to enjoy many years of undisturbed happiness in the possession of each other's love (which no one can take from us) and society. He visited my favourite rose, and found it flourishing in the highest beauty; and those near the windows are now as high as the parent tree. I long to see them, and to get a smile through the window while dressing from my beloved Philip. I hope I may allow myself to think of those joys with greater certainty than for so many years I have ever dared to do. Admiral Martin most kindly wrote me two or three days ago that the *Nova Scotia* was about to sail from Plymouth with despatches to Halifax, and that he would forward them for me. As I do not see by the papers that the ship *has* sailed, I shall still take my chance, and send this to him. I have not had a second letter from dear Mrs. Broke. I received a few hurried lines from her on Wednesday, when she had merely heard the telegraphic account that was forwarded to the Admiralty from Plymouth, and inserted the following day in the papers, which also added that you had brought your prize home safe into *that* port. She therefore only wrote to express her joy, and supposed that we had left this place and were all enjoying your loved society there. Mrs. Jenny and Ann were staying with her at Needham, which I am glad of. She, with my father and mother and brother, and indeed all our friends, far and near, have written and begged me to offer you their sincere congratulations. You cannot imagine how much kindness I have experienced from Admiral and Mrs. Sutton. I shall ever remember it with gratitude. I go to them upon all occasions for *relief* and advice, which they kindly afford me. Our dear children are all charmingly.

I shall take dear Philip back to Ottery this first week in August; he is naturally very anxious, dear boy, that the *Shannon* should return before that time, that he may accompany us to Plymouth, which I have promised in that case. Louisa, Willy, and George are, I flatter myself, benefited by change of air. Dear baby is now dipped in the sea every other day, which, I trust, will strengthen him; he does not at all dislike it. I shall take the liberty of enclosing this to the Commissioner, with my grateful thanks for his very kind attentions to you. Admirals Sawyer, Martin, Mrs. Justine, and numbers of others, have offered their gratulations. God bless you, my beloved husband! Our dear children unite in kindest love and kisses with your ever faithful and affectionate—

" Loo."

Captain Broke was sufficiently recovered by October to re-embark, and the *Shannon* having been ordered home, Broke invited Wallis to be his guest for the passage. On the 11th of that month they left Halifax for England. Even this voyage was not unattended with danger, for it was fully expected that Commodore Rodgers, in the *President*, would attempt to waylay them. Admiral King, in his Recollections, observes that Captain Broke, on resuming command of the *Shannon* to bring her home,

9

told his men the *President* might waylay him, and what he would do, and what they must do, if the *Shannon* fell in with her. He adds that, "As the *Shannon* had a convoy of eight dull-sailing merchant craft under her orders, and as everything done and intended to be done at Halifax was known in America through the Halifax newspapers, Rodgers had full and exact information, and therefore he must have known the day and very hour when to sail out of port to throw himself in the route of the *Shannon*. It is possible, however, that his government did not wish to *run the risk*; they were 'pretty considerably' damped by the capture of the *Chesapeake*."

Even during this voyage Captain Broke continued some of the old exercises to which his crew were accustomed, and assiduously prepared himself for a probable encounter with a French or American foe. None such, however, crossed his track, and after a stormy passage the *Shannon*, with her convoy, anchored at Spithead on November 3rd.

Broke and Wallis started in company for London the same afternoon, journeying as far as Liphook that evening, the next day to Guildford, and the third into London, Broke not being in a fit state to do more than a few miles a day. Wallis says he was very glad when Broke was quietly lodged at Limmer's Hotel, Conduit Street.

Taking up Wallis's own story, he says: "A day or two after, he (Broke) presented me to Lord Melville, then first Lord of the Admiralty, and, when he had recovered the fatigue of the journey, we retraced our steps to Portsmouth by the same easy stages, and having seen him safely back and comfortably lodged, where Lady Broke joined him, my care of him ended. Having bade each other a fervent farewell, I parted from a man that I loved most sincerely, and from whom I had, during nearly two years, received, I can truly say, *affectionate regard.* I also believe it to have been owing to his high bearing and sterling worth, added to the kindness of his government, that our crew were doubly incited to achieve under him a victory he had set his heart upon."

VII.

FATES OF THE "SHANNON" AND "CHESAPEAKE."

CHAPTER VII.

BEFORE me as I write is an inkstand bearing the following inscription : " This Inkstand is made from wood of the *Chesapeake*, captured by the *Shannon* June 1st, 1813. The capstan is made out of a beam of the *Shannon*." This capstan, which forms the reservoir for the ink, is a dense and perfectly sound piece of wood, though nearly ninety years have passed since the oaks of which the *Shannon* was constructed nodded and fell beneath the woodman's axe. She was built in 1806 at Chatham, on the Medway, by Thomas Brindley, whose firm of Thomas & Joseph Brindley also built many of the vessels which fought in the battle of Algiers ; and it may be mentioned here that one of the Admiral's correspondents, after he had passed his hundredth year, was a great-grandson of this same Thomas Brindley.

Two ships, each bearing the name of the *Shannon,* had previously been lost: one a 32-gun frigate, constructed in 1796, and wrecked in 1800; another of 36 guns, launched in 1803, and in the same year run aground under the batteries of Cape La Hogue.

The third, the *Shannon* of the present history, —name dear to every Briton—was a plain, massive, and effective ship, strictly of her class. She saw but little active service after her famous action, and, sound as she was, might well have lasted a century at least; but after she had been put to sundry " base uses," and had her name changed to that of the *St. Lawrence,* she was broken up some thirty years since, and many of her timbers were kindly presented by the Admiralty to Sir George Broke-Middleton, the then sole surviving son of her famous captain. They could until recently have been, and may perhaps still be, seen in the grounds of Broke Hall, Nacton, in the shape of an elegant pair of lofty gates.

For a number of years the *Shannon* was an object of considerable attraction, and as late as 1833 Admiral Sir John Beresford wrote from Sheerness to Sir Philip Broke: "I show the dear old *Shannon* as a ' lion ' here."

The accompanying illustration shows the figure-head of the *Shannon* in its present resting-place at Broke Hall, where it is carefully preserved with other

FIGURE HEAD OF H.M.S. 'SHANNON'

AND STAR FROM ''CHESAPEAKE'S' QUARTER (NOW IN ARCADE AT BROKE HALL).

From a Photograph by Mr. Cobb, of Ipswich.

relics of the fight. The star at the top is one of two carried by the *Chesapeake.* On one was the letter " U," on the other the letter " S," to represent United States. The star with the " U " upon it was destroyed by shot.

She is gone! but how far more truly than of Dido may it be said of her by all gallant hearts :—

"In freta dum fluvii current, dum montibus umbræ
Lustrabunt convexa, polus dum sidera pascet ;
Semper honos, nomenque tuum, laudesque manebunt." ·

The end of the *Chesapeake* was widely different. Pride of the American navy as she was, she proved of little service to our own, for naval architecture was taking a new turn. She was brought to England in 1815 by Captain F. Newcombe, in 1816 was in ordinary, and in 1820 was sold to Mr. Holmes, at Portsmouth, and broken up. Sold by our economical Government for £500, having been purchased seven years before for over £21,000!

The *Chesapeake* was built in 1797, at Norfolk, Virginia, and cost over £60,000. All her guns had names, engraven on small squares of copper-plate. The following list of twenty-five of them, on one side, has been preserved :—

1. Brother Jonathan.
2. True Blue.
3. Yankee Protection.

4. Putman.
5. Raging Eagle.
6. Viper.
7. General Warren.
8. Mad Anthony.
9. America.
10. Washington.
11. Liberty for Ever.
12. Dreadnought.
13. Defiance.
14. Liberty or Death.

(All these were 18-pounders.)

FORECASTLE.

15. United Tars.
16. Jumping Billy.⎫
17. Rattler.　　　　⎬ (32-pounders.)

QUARTERDECK.

18. Bull Dog.
19. Spitfire.
20. Nancy Dawson.
21. Revenge.
22. Bunker's Hill.
23. Pocahontas.
24. Towser.
25. Wilful Murder.

(All 32-pounders.)

Many years since, while I was making investigations in connection with the memoir of Sir Philip Broke, it was reported to me that the *Chesapeake* had been converted into a flour-mill, and was still in existence as such at Wickham, in Hampshire. I ventured to address some inquiries on the subject to the Vicar of Fareham, who courteously returned the following valuable reply:—

"FAREHAM VICARAGE, HANTS, *April 9th*, 1864.

" DEAR SIR,—

" I had never heard any of the interesting information about the *Chesapeake*, which you have conveyed to me, till your letter, received this morning, set me inquiring.

" Wickham is four miles north of Fareham, a district parish, the same place which gave birth to William of Wykeham. The *Chesapeake* was brought to Portsmouth (nine miles from hence) and was never used in the British navy. She was sold by Government to Mr. Holmes for £500, who found he had made a capital investment on this occasion, and cleared £1000 profit. He broke up the vessel, took several tons of copper from her, and disposed of the timbers, which were quite new and sound, of beautiful pitch pine, for building purposes. Much of the wood was employed in building houses in Portsmouth; but a large portion was sold in 1820 to

Mr. John Prior, a miller, of Wickham, for nearly £200. Mr. Prior pulled down his own mill at Wickham and constructed a new one with this timber, which he found admirably adapted for the purpose. The deck timbers were thirty-two feet long and eighteen inches square, and were placed, unaltered, horizontally in the mill. The purloins of the deck were about twelve feet long, and served without alteration for joists. The mill is still in existence and in active operation (the property of Mr. Goderick), stands just as Mr. Prior erected it in 1820, and is likely to last yet hundreds of years.

"Mr. Prior is now living in Fareham, and I have just taken the foregoing information from his lips.

"I remain, dear Sir,

"Very faithfully yours,

"W. S. Dumergue."

The receipt of this letter gave me an irresistible longing to see for myself the strange metamorphosis of a sanguinary man-of-war into a peaceful, life-sustaining flour-mill. It should have been a summer's day when I determined to make my pilgrimage, and *was* marked July in the calendar; but a more unceasing downpour of rain I never remember. Arriving at Fareham, a change of vehicle conveyed me more slowly through an undulating, picturesque, and well-wooded district. By-and-bye a valley opened, through which a stream might be conjectured to flow; and after a few turns more the " fly," with a grating check, drew up before a comely house of three stories with a range of dormer windows in the roof.

Nothing shiplike or of the sea was discernible from without. A young Englishman of some eight-and-twenty years of age was coming forth to join his cricket club on a neighbouring down (for the weather at last was beginning to brighten up a little), and this proved to be the master and owner of Chesapeake Mill. In a few words I told the errand which had led me so far from home, and was at once cordially and hospitably welcomed. Mr. Goderick was to some extent aware of the historical associations connected with his property, and on the sideboard in his dining-room was standing a large cigar-box, constructed from the polished pine of the old ship, and bearing the inscription " *Chesapeake* " in small brass nails.

After a brief interval I was shown the interior of the mill. The beams, joists, and floors were all constructed from the timber of the American frigate, and some of them were in many places pockmarked with shot. The mill, armed with many modern appliances, was merrily going; and on every floor the blithe and mealy men were urging their toil. Thought I, on one of these planks, beyond reasonable doubt, brave Lawrence fell, in the writhing anguish of his mortal wound ; on another, if not the same, Watt's head was carried away by grapeshot ; and on others, Broke lay, ensanguined, and his assailants dead ! Thus pondering I stood, and still the busy men went on, corn passed beneath the stones, and flour—agent of mortal life— poured forth, while merry millers passed around their kindly smile and blithesome jest.

Perhaps, thought I, at last, it is better this should be the end of the proud *Chesapeake.* The dream of glory (and never was one more lofty) lives, and long shall live, upon the page of history ; but one day of this tranquil toil in God's holy name and love would, I think, be infinitely more valued by Philip Broke now than would the capture of a thousand *Chesapeakes,* for he is hard on the confines of that glorious land where, in the sublime language of the sacred prophet, "Shall go no galley with oars, neither shall gallant ship pass thereby"; and where nations shall make war no more.

VIII.

WALLIS'S FURTHER SERVICES AND APPOINTMENTS.

CHAPTER VIII.

FROM 1813 Commander Wallis, as he now was, continued his upward progress in his noble profession, until (as I am sure he would be himself the first to say) he had, *by God's kind providence,* attained the summit of rank and the extreme limit of mortal years—one hundred and——. Happily I have not yet to fill up the blank. The records of his further services, now so distant, must of necessity be scanty, more especially as he never kept journals, nor, indeed, saved much of his correspondence; but such details as I am now able to give will, I trust, prove accurate.

Very soon after his return to England in the *Shannon,* viz., on January 19th, 1814, he was appointed to the 12-gun sloop *Snipe,* and served in her at Sheerness until December 28th following. He was advanced to post rank on August 12th, 1819, but until his appointment to the *Niemen,* 28, on June 4th, 1824,

10

had no active employment. With this ship he remained until November 1826, and in her commanded the first experimental squadron, consisting of the *Champion, Orestes, Pylades, Calliope,* and *Algerine.* He was employed on his old station at Halifax, and it was during this period, as I have explained, that Wallis was most sumptuously entertained at Boston as an officer of the old *Shannon,* some reference to which circumstance will be found in the following letter from his old captain, then Sir Philip B. V. Broke :—

"BROKE HALL, *December 24th,* 1826.

"DEAR WALLIS,—

"I am very full of county business, and with a head that aches with any writing or application ; but I must thank you for your kind letter and obliging and gratifying communications. As you account for your return it is all very satisfactory, and I trust will answer all expectations. 'Tis good to oblige some people, and I hope you will find it so when you apply for another employ. You may then take a turn where freights are moving, and so lay in a little of that mineral ballast that is so useful when we are laid up in ordinary.

"If any circumstance brings you this way, we shall be very happy to see you here, and chat over past adventures. It is pleasing to find our cousin *Jonathan* has so much hearty *English* good humour in him, thus to shake hands and be friendly when the battle is over. I daresay they looked at little *Niemen* with much interest, as a representative of their old *playfellow* the *Shannon.*

" I was glad to hear your good admiral was so well, and was such a friend of yours, for I have a great esteem for him, and value his good opinion highly. My brother has just left me to go with the army to Portugal, and Philip * is there—at Lisbon, in the *Genoa*—very happy, and amusing himself in spite of the rebels. My second boy, George, is in the *Glasgow*, up the archipelago, equally amused with hunting Greek pirates and looking at antiquities. You say nothing of your wife and children, but I hope they are all well, and, with yourself, will enjoy many happy returns of this genial season. I remain a useless invalid and unfit for sea service, though I get out more than I did, by *immense* clothing on my cold side ; and Lady Broke has also rather more liberty, but is still carried up and down stairs, which is a great inconvenience and confinement. She unites in regards to you and in compliments to Mrs. Wallis with,

<blockquote>
" My dear shipmate,
" Yours most truly,
" P. B. V. BROKE."
</blockquote>

* Admiral Sir Philip Broke's son.

Captain Wallis now had a good many years' rest from active employment, as it was not until April 14th, 1838, that he again took a command. He was then appointed to the *Madagascar*, 46, in which ship he remained until September 1839. During this service he was employed with other British ships at Vera Cruz, when that town was surprised and bombarded by a French squadron, under Admiral Baudin, in December 1838. Wallis did excellent service here in protecting the interests of the British merchants, who gave him special thanks.

Some four years again elapsed without Wallis taking a command, and during this interval the distressing news of the death of his old captain, of the *Shannon*, was communicated to him by the following letter :—

"Broke Hall, *January 8th*, 1841.

"My dear Wallis,—

"Before this reaches you the newspapers will have announced that it has pleased Providence to deprive me of the kindest and best of fathers. He was in town previously, for two months, for the purpose of obtaining surgical advice, and, till three days before his death, no danger was apprehended. This blow, therefore, comes very suddenly on my poor mother and sister and all his relations. It is a consolation to me to have been with him in his last moments, and to know that few men leave this world better prepared than he was to submit with resignation and submission to the Divine will. The funeral will take place here to-morrow, and will be strictly private, in order that my poor mother and sister may not be unnecessarily shocked by the sad ceremony being prolonged.

" *You* will, I know, condole with me; and believe me,

" Dear Wallis,

" Yours ever truly,

" P. BROKE."

There was not, perhaps, any one outside the deceased Admiral's own circle who felt his loss more keenly than did Wallis. To him he had been more than a comrade in arms—more than a friend—he had been a man whom Wallis revered and loved.

On October 13th, 1843, Wallis took the command of the *Warspite*, 50, a ship of which he was very fond. In her he was employed in the Mediterranean during the French-Morocco war, and witnessed the attack on Tangier and destruction of Mogador by the French squadron, which happened respectively on August 6th and 15th, 1844. On the latter occasion he was the senior British officer present, and in addition to being complimented by numerous officials, received the thanks of the British and French Governments for the judicious arrangements made by him, in his quasi-diplomatic character, with the Prince de Joinville, under whose command the French squadron was, and who added his personal thanks to those of his Government. It was largely due to the tact Wallis displayed on this occasion that an out break of war with France was avoided.

Wallis was also the senior British officer present during the civil war on the coast of Syria throughout the whole of the year 1845, he being then still in command of the *Warspite* ; and here again he was specially thanked by Capitan Pasha, and our Minister and Consul-General at Constantinople.

In 1847 Wallis was offered a good-service pension, which he declined, and was then appointed a naval aide-de-camp to the Queen. This honourable post he held until 1851, when he was promoted to flag rank. It was not, however, until April 1st, 1857, that he hoisted his flag, which he did on board the *Cumberland*, 70, and then proceeded to the south-east coast of America as Commander-in-chief on that coast.

In the following year he was recalled, in consequence of his having been promoted to the rank of Vice-Admiral in the previous September, and arrived at Spithead on August 4th, 1858, not afterwards to go afloat in the service of his country. Little more, indeed, could be expected of him, for he was nearly seventy years of age, and had, with some intervals of rest, been actively employed for fifty-four years. It was, in fact, owing to the length and nature of his

SIR PROVO WALLIS

AT THE AGE OF SIXTY.

services, that when the great retirement in the navy took place it was decided, at the suggestion of Mr. Childers, then the First Lord of the Admiralty, and by a special Order in Council, that his name should be retained on the active list of flag officers for the rest of his life as a special mark of distinction. On that list it still stands, and for many years past it has been, and is now, at the head of the list. It is compulsory on admirals of the fleet to retire at the age of seventy, and the honour which Admiral Wallis enjoys in being on the active list, notwithstanding his advanced age, is unique.

To complete our hero's list of honours, it must be mentioned that he was created a K.C.B. on May 18th, 1860; made Admiral in March 1863; created G.C.B. in 1873, and made Admiral of the Fleet in December 1877. He was Rear-Admiral of the United Kingdom from 1869 to 1870, and from that time to 1876 Vice-Admiral of the United Kingdom, the last-mentioned honour being one of which he was very proud, and which he relinquished with regret on his appointment to Admiral of the Fleet.

Such then, briefly told, is the public career of that very young midshipman with whom I started, and whose progress I have traced until his attainment of the highest possible rank that his profession could give. I will endeavour later, by the help of his correspondence, to show that his private life has been one which merits our admiration as much as his brave exploits on the ocean.

IX.

FAMILY CIRCLE.

CHAPTER IX.

FAMILY CIRCLE.

IT has been already shown that Sir Provo had no
brother, but he had three sisters, the eldest of
whom (Elizabeth) I have already referred to as attending upon Captain Broke during his illness at Halifax,
consequent upon the wounds he had received in the
Shannon's duel with the *Chesapeake*. This sister, as
I have explained, was then the wife of Captain Lord
James Townshend, R.N., K.C.H., to whom she was
married in May 1813. Having been left a widow,
Lady Townhsend in 1844 again married, her second
husband being Captain William Honeyman Henderson, R.N., C.B., who commanded the *Gorgon* at the
bombardment of Sidon and St. Jean d'Acre. She died
in July 1872, after having lived to a good old age.

Sir Provo's second sister, Maria, died unmarried.

His third and youngest sister, Mary, was married to the Rev. Dennis George Norris, Vicar of Kessingland, Suffolk, and died in 1844, leaving children, some of whom are, I think, now living.

Sir Provo was married on October 19th, 1817, to Juliana, second daughter of the Venerable Roger Massey, Archdeacon of Barnstaple and Prebendary of Exeter, and two daughters were born of this marriage but no son. He was left a widower, and on July 21st, 1849, married his second wife, the present Lady Wallis, who was a daughter of the late distinguished General Sir Robert Thomas Wilson, M.P., Governor of Gibraltar. Of this marriage there has been no issue.

Sir Provo's eldest daughter was, like his eldest sister, named Elizabeth, and was married in October 1858 to the Rev. Doctor Perryn, of Trafford Hall, near Chester, who died suddenly, at Oxford, on January 19th, 1878, at the age of fifty-three. Sir Provo, although he was then eighty-seven years of age, went to that city immediately on hearing of his daughter's bereavement to offer such consolation as he could afford, but he says that the shock to him was great. Mrs. Perryn was spared for many years, and died as recently as January 2nd, 1890, at the age of seventy-two. Sir Provo's second daughter is still living, and has never been married.

Lady Wallis has herself exceeded life's allotted span by many years, having been born in 1807. As will be seen from Sir Provo's letters, which follow, she has for a long time past been an invalid; but her sufferings have been so lightened by the anxious care bestowed upon her by her husband, that happiness has reigned where sorrow might have been suspected to have found a resting-place. Need I add, that in his wife's love and reciprocal solicitude, Sir Provo has found a great reward for his goodness.

X.

CORRESPONDENCE.

CHAPTER X.

CORRESPONDENCE.

THE following extracts from letters received by me from Sir Provo, and the first of which was written nearly thirty years ago, will, it is hoped, be interesting, not only because they will show Sir Provo's personality more clearly to the reader, but also because they prove that notwithstanding his great age his faculties have been marvellously well retained. What is perhaps more wonderful is the fact that every one of these letters, even that written after the Admiral had passed the hundredth year of his age, was entirely written by himself, in a firm and legible hand. Indeed, these letters are unique as specimens of caligraphy, when the age of the writer is considered. A fac-simile reproduction of his last letter to me will be found further on ; but it should be mentioned here

11

that, as a specimen of the Admiral's writing, it does not favourably compare with the letters written by him in 1889, when he was close on ninety-eight years of age.

The first letter received by me from Sir Provo was that set out in the preface to this volume, which opened a friendship that has endured without interruption .until the present time, and increased in fervour year by year.

In making these extracts, an endeavour will be made not to repeat what has already been set out in earlier parts of the present volume.

"*Funtington, January* 26*th*, 1864.—No doubt you have kindly attributed my silence to indisposition (such is the fact) ; and I am sorry to tell you that the day after my agreeable interview with you in London, I was seized with influenza, which caused my immediate return home, since which I have been a great sufferer, caused by heavy cold and an attack of gout in both legs. It is only to-day that I have felt equal to the least exertion, and avail myself of the power to thank you for your most friendly letter of the 19th inst., and to add that I will, as soon as possible, send you the memoranda you have asked for."

"*Funtington, February* 19*th*, 1864.—I write a line from my bed to thank you for your kind sympathy, and also for having sent me your photograph, which I shall value, though, like all others of the sort, it gives too severe an expression. However, having had the pleasure of seeing you, I retain a much more agreeable impression of your countenance. Immediately after my last letter I was under the necessity of again taking to my bed, and am still keeping it, owing to gout in both feet and right ankle. Influenza has also left me very feeble, and I very much regret to find that you have not yet quite got rid of that uncomfortable malady."

" *Funtington, March* 16*th*, 1864.—Should the enclosed memoranda * be of any use to you, glean from it what you please. I am indeed sorry that I have not any map or diagram to send you, but, had I not been prevented by illness, it was my intention to have consulted the *Shannon's* Log Book at Somerset House for site of engagement. As no evolutions were performed during the action, the positions of the ships were exactly what the late Admiral King's pictures delineate. You have, I think, a copy of Broke's certificate to me, and the following is a copy of his note when he sent me a sword. (*This note is given on p.* 128). All I can say of the late Sir Charles Falkiner is, that he was an excellent messmate and as gallant a fellow as ever lived. I appointed him prize-master of the *Chesapeake*, and he conducted her into the harbour of Halifax highly to my satisfaction. We never after served together."

---

* With reference to the *Shannon* and *Chesapeake* action.

"*Funtington, March 21st*, 1864.—I omitted to mention that a schooner accompanied the *Chesapeake* from the port of Boston, with merchants and others on board to see the fight, and hove to out of gunshot to windward of us. I will look over O'Byrne's biography, and correct the errors, and shall be happy to give you any other information in my power, but fifty years and upwards is a long while (without notes) to tax memory; however, the little I have told you I can vouch for."

"*Funtington, September 12th*, 1864.—I am more annoyed than I can express by the delay that has occurred in obtaining the information you asked me for, and now, after having waited so long, I find that the person who was to do the needful at Somerset House is away for his holidays; however, if our original Log contains no greater amount of information than the extract you sent me, I fear the bearing and distance of lighthouse at the specified time were not inserted, and if not, I think it quite sufficient to state that it took place (viz., hoisting the ensign and firing the gun) when within about three miles of the lighthouse. Many thanks for the photograph of the mill * which you sent, and for two others which have recently arrived. I have been a great wanderer of late, which is an additional reason for not having communicated with you sooner."

* The mill constructed out of the remains of the *Chesapeake*.

"*Funtington, September 22nd,* 1864.—I have at length heard from Staff-Commander Thomas, of the Admiralty, who has sent me the enclosed memo. from *Shannon's* Log, which is all he can glean; and I much regret not having any of my own to add, as I was not in the habit of recording occurrences. The extract which you have from *Shannon's* Log is verbatim, and is (as I before mentioned) a meagre affair, though easily accounted for, as we had not a master at that period, so it was kept by one of our midshipmen (Mr. Etough), who had at the time an acting order as master; but ships' Logs in those days rarely contained any matter beyond a careless record of events, and ditto weather, and for myself I confess to not having had anything to do with it, as I had so many other anxious duties that pressed upon me. But I well remember that *Chesapeake* was at anchor in Nantasket Roads when we first saw her on June 1st, and that Boston Light is upon an outer island, the name of which I do not remember. I have had several very kind letters from Sir George,* and have sent him (as requested) a photograph in uniform."

"*Funtington, November 15th,* 1864.—Many thanks for photograph of my old shipmate Sweeney.† There

---

* Admiral Sir George Broke-Middleton.

† Sweeney at this time had become a master barber on the banks of the Liffey, and often did me the honour of trimming my beard while he was "yarning" about the *Shannon's* fight. I lost sight of him about 1868, and do not remember to have heard of his death.—J. G. B.

can be but few of the 'old *Shannons*' left. Of the officers none but myself, as Major Law of the Marines (our then second lieutenant in that corps) died last month, and on the 20th inst. I had the melancholy satisfaction of attending his remains to the grave. There is, however, one other officer who was in our action still living, retired Commander George Raymond,* but he did not belong to the *Shannon*, we having recaptured him. *Belle Poule* was his ship."

"*Funtington, November 21st*, 1864.—As to Captain Raymond's address, I will get it for you should it still be your wish, though I think his memory is not very accurate, as I found out some little time ago from a letter he addressed to me."

"*Funtington, June 1st*, 1865.—I shall not attempt to express all I feel for your kind congratulations, just received, on the anniversary of *Shannon's* action, but be assured your warmth of heart, apparent in every line, has deeply penetrated mine. I saw Broke Middleton in London this spring."

"*Scarsdale Villa, Great Malvern, June 16th*, 1865.—We are not leaving Malvern just yet, and I can assure you it will give me great pleasure to see

---

* Commander Raymond lived until about two years after the date of this letter, and died at the age of 71.—J. G. B.

you here. When you have fixed the day pray let me
know, or perhaps I might be as unfortunate as when
you kindly ran down to Sydenham."

" *Funtington, March 26th*, 1866.—I have received
from Sir Broke-Middleton a copy of your work,*
which has relieved my mind, for I feared you might
be ill, *owing to delay in publication.* I shall read the
memoir with melancholy pleasure, and also with deep
gratitude to you for the high opinion you have so
kindly formed of me. Should anything bring you to
England it would give me great pleasure to see you
here."

" *Funtington, June 2nd*, 1866.—I am much pleased
to hear of an intended second edition.† Another is
required to correct a few inaccuracies as to Commander Raymond's statement that Lieutenant Ludlow
died on board *Chesapeake.* I simply reply, *not true.*
The poor fellow was brought on board the *Shannon*
immediately after the action, and was placed in poor
Watt's cabin, where I daily visited him until we sent
him to Halifax Hospital, and he *died there* about a
week (certainly some days) after our arrival. The fact
is, he was not on board his own ship for an hour after
the action. Secondly, I can only say that the story

* The author's Memoir of Admiral Sir P. B. V. Broke.
† This refers to the same Memoir.

of ' an attempt to recapture *Chesapeake* whilst the *Shannons* were reefing topsails,' was never reported to me by Lieutenant Falkiner, who was in charge of her. I am very glad you have consulted Commander Raymond, though his memory certainly seems very *defective*. I will gladly answer any questions you may think proper to put to me ; pray *do not hesitate*. I return to Malvern at the end of ensuing week, and to the same quarters where you kindly visited me. Your letter luckily got here just as I arrived home (for a few days only). I left Lady Wallis under Gully's care. Are you to be in Worcestershire this summer P I think you told me it was your intention. If so, I will readily wait upon you, when I hear of your whereabouts."

" *Funtington*, *May* 24*th*, 1867.—Years do indeed ' glide by,' but by the goodness of Providence you and I are still spared. You have of late had a trying time to go through, and I grieve to think that although ' the plague ' is stayed, Ireland is not content ; so we must hope for better government. My wife, thank God ! keeps fairly well, and if by keeping strictly to Gully's rules health can be secured, she deserves success. At this moment I cannot say whether we shall be at Malvern this year, and it is lucky we are not there now, as it is complete wintry weather, and is less bearable from being unnatural. Are you likely to be in London this year P And if so, would you come and see us? I have only a warm reception to offer, but, believe me, it would afford us the *greatest pleasure.*

" *Funtington, October* 12*th,* 1867.—I am happy to tell you that Providence has kindly supported me amidst my many trials, and that my bruised sister * is doing as well as we can expect at her age (seventy-three) ; the other, I hope, is in heaven. Pray accept once more my grateful thanks for your kind sympathy. As to Politics and Fenianism, it appears that we are not to be long without trouble. Universal discord seems to be the order of the day, and the state of our Church is the cause of much sorrow to many."

" *Funtington, January* 21*st,* 1868.—I am glad to hear that the books from Mr. Randolph have reached you safely. By them you will find that Sir R. W. † was not an ordinary character ; in fact, he lived in most illiberal days, when the vengeance of king and ministry always crushed those, if possible, who differed in opinion from them, and even suborned others *to lie.* However, Sir R.'s memory will live, and posterity will do him justice, whilst many another is doomed to oblivion. How glad I should be to show you many documents that I have, wherein crowned

---

* Mrs. Henderson, his eldest sister.
† The late General Sir Robert Wilson—Lady Wallis's father.

heads, and other leading men in Europe, have expressed their opinion of the gallantry and greatness of mind of my lamented father-in-law. Had there been at the R. headquarters in those days 'our own correspondent,' things would have been better understood by our countrymen."

"*Funtington, April 25th*, 1868.—It would indeed give me much pleasure to spend another day with you at Ombersley this summer, but there is not a chance of our being at Malvern so early in the year, as I have to go into Norfolk and Cheshire upon business. Mr. Featherstonhaugh's assassination is indeed a sad affair, and was no doubt a great shock to you. I trust that the Royal visit to Ireland may do some good, though I fear there is not much hope for your distracted country."

"*Scarsdale, Great Malvern, December 21st*, 1868. —We came to Malvern on the 12th of last month (and are in our old quarters), and may remain perhaps until March. What events have taken place since you and I met here—surely our national decadency has fairly set in! (More rapidly than I expected.) The wolves in sheep's clothing within our fold are chuckling, but may God upset their plans. We are at present a divided people, and Ritualism is making rapid progress, and our bishops without power to meet it."

" *Funtington, April* 15*th*, 1869.—I have been from home, and, since my return, very busy with workmen in the house. We returned from Malvern last month, after a sojourn of nearly four months, and I trust my wife is benefited by ' the treatment.' I sympathise with you respecting poor Ireland, and my first cousin, Doctor Lee, Rector of Ahoghill, has exerted himself strenuously in the good cause, but with little success."

" *Funtington, August* 17*th*, 1869.—I hope ere this you are finding things better in Ireland than you anticipated, but where ' Romans ' abound their motto, ' *Aut Cæsar aut nullus*,' will ever prevail. P.S.— Should it not have met your eye, you will be pleased to hear that I have been made ' Rear-Admiral of the United Kingdom.' "

" *Funtington, December* 13*th*, 1869.—Your letter of the 9th only reached me yesterday (Sunday), and to-day I am preparing for a trip to town upon business. I merely mention this to ensure your pardoning my hasty scrawl. It has given me much concern to hear that you have had a serious attack of sciatica, only mitigated by your telling me that you are approaching convalescence. May the waters of Droitwich counteract the poisonous medicine which you have been dosed with. Thanks, my good friend (heartfelt), for all your good wishes, and may you and yours enjoy all earthly happiness, and, when it shall please God to take us,

may we be received where pain and sorrow are unknown. The last sand in my glass of life is drawing
to an end. May you see many more years ; and should
they prove what I desire, you will indeed be happy.
Your situation in Ireland must indeed be grievous, but
what can be done for your unhappy country ? Our
statesmen are upon the horns of a dilemma, and I
fear we have not seen the last of the drama. Melancholy indeed is the prospect before us, with a *divided
Church* ; and if Parliament does not soon act and
crush *Puseyism*, evil will shortly come upon us. We
live in perilous days, but God, I trust, will guard the
just ; so prays yours, I may say, affectionately,—Provo
Wallis."

" *Funtington, July* 14*th*, 1870.—As you have
always expressed such friendly feelings towards me, I
am sure you will pardon my vanity in communicating
my appointment as ' Vice-Admiral of the United
Kingdom,' a much coveted honour in our profession."

" *Funtington, June* 6*th*, 1871.—I was from home
when your most kind letter of the 29th ult. reached
here, or I should not have delayed thus long in thanking
you warmly for your ever thoughtful remembrance of
' the memorable day.' "

" *Funtington, March* 8*th*, 1872.—Your letter of
February 28th arrived in due course at Funtington,

but I had previously fled into Norfolk, having been called there by the serious illness of my only sister, who is in a declining state. I only returned home yesterday. The melancholy death of Lord Mayo must have shocked you. Fortunately I had not the pleasure of his acquaintance."

" *Funtington, May* 28*th*, 1872.—I must no longer delay replying to your valued letter which I received some days since, or the anniversary of the day in question will have come and gone. I can hardly believe that it is fifty-nine years since that event, and that I am the only officer left. It gave me great pleasure to hear that your native air had restored you to health. Long may you enjoy this blessing upon earth, and when you are removed may eternal happiness be your lot. I am not, I fear, sufficiently thankful for the great mercies I have received, but He who is all goodness knows that I am grateful. We do not intend visiting Malvern this season, as my dear wife thinks she will not require further *punishment* this year."

" *Funtington, May* 26*th*, 1873.—From my heart I thank you for your kind congratulations, but especially for your prayers. Sixty years have passed like a dream since the Almighty was pleased to spare me, and I believe that I am the only survivor who was in that action—certainly the only officer. I beg you to excuse this scrawl, as I have, in consequence of my advancement to G.C.B., a score of letters to answer."

" *Scarsdale, Great Malvern, September 22nd,* 1873.—An abominable cold has kept me mostly in bed ever since I saw you. However, thank God, I am better, and scribble a few lines to tell you that, having business to attend to both at home and in London, it is my intention to leave this for about a fortnight on Friday next, stopping at Oxford *en route* a day or two. As to *Cleopatra's* action, my dear doctor, I was then a mere child, fourteen years old ; but looking back, I think it was a most chivalrous fight. I think I am the only surviving soul."

" *Scarsdale, Great Malvern, October 20th,* 1873. —I duly received your letter of the 16th, enclosing your photograph, which I think an excellent likeness, and be assured it will often give me pleasure when I look upon it, and think of the friend it represents. I have forwarded to-day a trifling *cadeau,* which pray accept, and place it upon your library table or elsewhere, in remembrance of one who feels highly honoured by the friendship you have bestowed upon him. After my return home, I will look for my late Captain's (Sir Robert Laurie) letter respecting *Cleopatra's* action."

"*Funtington, December* 15*th*, 1873.—I feel more than I can express, but heartily thank you for your kind congratulations upon my recent visit *to Windsor.* May I beg the favour of your not buying a ' Peerage ' for next year, as I ordered an extra one, hoping you would do me the favour of accepting it."

"*Funtington, March* 10*th*, 1874.—My dear wife's health renders her completely unable to enjoy society. I merely mention this to account for my inhospitable conduct, and to add how much I wish it were otherwise. I am much gratified by the Conservatives having returned to office, and I hope they will have a long lease of power. Worcester certainly disgraced herself, and no doubt it annoyed you. I think the Tichborne trial a great reflection upon our courts of law."

"*Funtington, October* 13*th*, 1874.—Time reminds me not to delay any longer sending you a few lines ; in fact, I have gone on day by day hoping to be able to tell you that the gout had taken its leave of me, but I am sorry to say it still clings, and, I fear, seems inclined to do so : at present I am free from acute pain, but cannot make a good walk—only a shuffle. I do hope, my dear friend, that you are keeping well, and I pray to God that you may, for without health we are poor creatures. My dear wife continues in an unsatisfactory state, though Dr. Quin, I think, has

done her some good. We often speak of you, and
I may say she feels very grateful for all your kind
and sympathetic feeling for us. As I write with a
crampy hand, I will only add our sincere wish that
you may continue to enjoy health and happiness."

"*Funtington, March 17th*, 1875.—No doubt you
have keenly felt the loss of your friends. I know full
well how sad are such feelings, but I think I am right
in saying you will bear, with Christian fortitude, the
decrees of Providence. I think I am gaining ground,
and hope to get to Malvern by-and-bye. If so, it will
give me the greatest pleasure to find you in *rude
health.* The weather still continues much against
invalids, and my dear wife does not, as sailors say,
make much, if any, headway."

"*Funtington, May 7th*, 1875.—I have been intending day by day to scribble you a line, but, as we used
to say at school, 'Procrastination is the thief of
time.' The sympathy you so kindly offered respecting Dr. Randolph's death was happily not required,
as it was not my brother-in-law; but your observa-
tions respecting survivorship are indeed true, for, like
yourself, I have to mourn the loss of nearly all my
dearest friends; but a person of my very advanced
years must expect such losses. *Apropos*, Mr. Randolph has just lost a cousin of his, *sixty-three years*
rector of Mint Haddam, in Hertfordshire, son of a

late Bishop of London. Previously to your communication of the death of your friend, Mr. Atkyns, I had seen it in the papers, which recalled to my memory the pleasant day we passed at Ombersley. Well do I remember the agreeable dinner you gave me, and the splendid salmon you had provided. With regard to your kind inquiries respecting our health, I wish it were in my power, my very dear friend, to tell you that we were free from ailments; but, indeed, we continue a brace of poor creatures, but not without hope, if we can get to Malvern, of being better. Unluckily we cannot get our old quarters, which is a bore; nevertheless, when we feel equal to the journey, we shall, no doubt, find a comfortable residence and be revived by its charming air."

"*Great Malvern, August 25th,* 1875.—I trust one day whilst here to again shake you by the hand, but shall not be able to do so on Saturday next. I promise myself the pleasure by-and-bye, when I feel more equal to moving about, to drive over from Worcester to Kington and have a few hours' gossip with you—I wish I could add, walk about with you. However, when we meet you will see that I can now only shuffle; but I am very grateful to Providence for granting me power to bring my dear wife here, who was in great want of a change of air, as well as to see the medical man, in whom she has great faith. But more of this when we meet."

"*Great Malvern, August* 28*th*, 1875.—God will-ing, to whom I pray for health and strength, I will with much pleasure accept your arrangement. Should it suit your convenience, let the day be Saturday, September 4th, when perhaps you may be able to accompany me to the Cathedral, as I should much like to have a look at the venerable building now that it has been recently beautified."

"*Great Malvern, October* 8*th*, 1875.—On Tuesday morning we shall slip our moorings and steer home-wards. When again (D.V.) we are settled at home, we hope to feel all the better for the change. At all events, it has given me the heartfelt pleasure of having visited Kington. I shall often dwell with pleasure upon my pleasant visit, and will never forget your hearty welcome. *Apropos*, the words of an old song intrude on my memory, viz. :

> ' And shall I then never revisit the spot,
> And steal through the village to gaze on the cot,
> Which clings to remembrance with fondest delay
> Through the dreams of the night and cares of the day ? '

But a truce to being sentimental, except to say that I intend, if possible, to attend to the impressive words I heard from your lips, ' Fret not thyself' ; and pray adhere to the same yourself. You, indeed, have a severe six months before you, and if I am spared shall often think I see you trudging in mud and slush. Give my kind regards to the good squire.* I thank you, my dear friend, for having made me acquainted with one so worthy. I send you an old *Court Calendar*, as a short paragraph caught my eye referring to Lord Beauchamp, which the squire has not seen ; therefore, when next you visit him, put the paper in your pocket and say I could not find the one which gave a more detailed account."

" *Funtington, October* 28*th,* 1875.—Thanks, my dear friend, for your kind offer should you go to Halifax in the spring ; but I believe, owing to the time which has elapsed since any steps were taken in the matter, that ' *Le jeu ne vaut pas la chandelle.*' You will have read, no doubt, of the death of Dr. Hook, Dean of Chichester—a man who will be greatly missed in this neighbourhood, as he was much liked. I hope his successor will not be a Ritualist. I occasionally look with pleasure at a young heifer, now nearly a yearling, which I intend for you when you get into your new rectory. My black-edged paper is owing to the death of a sister-in-law, widow of a late Rector of Barrow, near Chester (John Clark)."

" *Funtington, April* 19*th,* 1876.—The time for your intended trip, I conclude, is fast approaching ; so not to trouble you when you are engaged with

* William Laslett, Esq., M.P. for Worcester.

other matters, I send you a few lines to wish you God-speed, and also to say I shall not fail to pray for your protection by Him during your absence, and also for a safe return to your home and friends, which I hope to be able to witness, and then once more press the hand of a dear friend ere we part for ever. *Ever,* did I say? I trust not, for God may, of His infinite mercy, permit us hereafter to meet where pain and sorrow are no more. What a season we have had ever since our last visit to Malvern, and we have both felt it severely, especially my beloved wife. I have made up my mind not to trouble you about my property in Nova Scotia, feeling certain that too much time has elapsed without my looking after it."

"*Funtington, June 6th,* 1876.—Many thanks for your affectionate letter of *June 1st,* to which I reply on the anniversary of the day upon which we anchored in Halifax Harbour. I enclose a letter of Broke-Middleton's, who asks me about his father's hat. What became of it I do not know, my thoughts at that time being occupied with pressing matter."

"*Great Malvern, November 3rd,* 1876.—So, as the saying is in Cheshire, you have been 'flitting' —may it be in every way a comfort to you. Poor Polly!* I fear she has been like the present of

---

* The heifer given to me by Sir Provo.—J. G. B.

a white elephant to you, but let us hope in the end she may reward your care with some rich food. We are going on in the same jog-trot way, but do not intend to leave until the end of the month."

" *Funtington, January 9th,* 1877.— Some time having elapsed since I heard from you, I begin to think that, like so many others at the present time, you are unwell. Pray let me have a line, as I am anxious to know how you are this horrid weather. What dreadful accounts the papers tell us have been received from all parts of the world. We have only occasionally seen the sun since our return from Malvern, and my dear wife has never been out of the house. She is, I am sorry to add, still tormented, in spite of Doctors Quin and Fernie. As you were kind enough to express a wish that Mr. Randolph should go on with the life of the late Sir Robert Wilson, I am sorry to say that he has informed me that his health is such that he cannot proceed with it, and has given the trustees of the British Museum many valuable manuscripts. I very much regret that this is so, as I should much have liked the world to have seen how very shamefully he had been treated by the Government of his day."

" *Funtington, April 10th,* 1877.— The secluded

life I lead prevents my having more to tell you than that we both continue great invalids. My dear wife has not been out of our own grounds since our return from Malvern, and I suffer a good deal with rheumatic gout. The political world is still looking very gloomy, and God only knows how things will settle down, as there seems much trouble brewing both at home and elsewhere."

"*Funtington, June 1st,* 1877.—Your kind letter of the 17th was duly received, by which you antici-pated that the Almighty would mercifully extend my life. Well, my dear friend, the 1st of June has once more returned, and although it finds me the worse for wear, I am better than I could have expected from my advanced age, for which I humbly offer up to the Giver of all good my grateful thanks. And now, my dear doctor, whilst thanking you very sincerely for all your good wishes, I cannot refrain from adding that I feel quite undeserving of the encomiums your friendship bestows upon me. I am glad to hear of the continued good health of your kind friend the squire, and from the tenor of your letter I conclude your own to be satisfactory. With respect to the miserable war now raging, I hope Providence will soon put a stop to it; but the state of affairs are such that mortal man cannot see through the mist. As I am writing with an unsatisfactory pen—like a skewer—I will call a halt, with our best and kindest wishes for all good ; ever affectionately yours, PROVO WALLIS.''

" *Funtington, September 12th*, 1877.—My dear wife, I regret to tell you, still remains a great invalid, and your humble servant, though not suffering acute pain, has a good deal of gout flying about him. Thanks for telling me ' Polly's ' doings in the butter way. How many weeks did it take her to give you 80 lbs.? I shall be glad to know, as I wish to compare the pasturage of your county with ours. However, you must wait until she has had her second calf, as she will not be in full profit until then.''

" *Great Malvern, November 2nd*, 1877.—I was very glad to hear that the good squire was himself again, but sorry to find that you were thinking of getting into your new *damp* rectory. If I knew the bishop, I would ask him to prohibit your doing so— indeed, my dear fellow, it will be a very wrong move, to run the risk of your life. My dear wife is slowly recovering from the effects of a long day's journey. I am, thank God, much as you found me last year, and by-and-bye we can arrange a meeting at Worcester. It is a bold stroke my coming here, but what won't a man do who loves his wife. We only got here late on Tuesday evening, and as I am now writing by owl's light, I must call a halt."

" *Funtington, February* 28*th,* 1878. — The late severe blow, by the loss of my son-in-law* (only in his fifty-fourth year), has been a great grief, and I hope you have been spared any similar pain. I am sorry to tell you my dear wife continues to be tormented, though her medical man at Malvern pronounced her free from the enemy. It is very sad for her, but we are all bound to submit to the will of Providence. As for myself, I am truly thankful, at my great age, to be so mercifully treated. My kind remembrances to the squire. What does he think of the ' Times ' ? "

" *Funtington, April* 23*rd,* 1878.—It is now some time since we exchanged ideas, nevertheless you have not been out of my thoughts, and more particularly so as I have had many severe bereavements, added to intense sorrow by the continued sufferings of my dear wife ; but I will not dwell upon sorrows or evils, but pray to the great God for mercy and forgiveness."

" *Funtington, June* 1*st,* 1878.—Time does indeed, as you observe, fly ; but, by God's mercy, I can once more send you my heartfelt thanks for your kind letter concerning this, to me, eventful day."

" *Great Malvern, July* 4*th,* 1878.—Being once more able to hold a pen, and you having kindly

* Dr. Perryn.

appointed me commander-in-chief, I take advantage
of my office by directing you, at present, to remain
quietly at your anchorage of Kington ; and when it
may please God to permit me to get to Worcester
comfortably, I hope the good squire will be able to
drive you there, and take a lunch dinner with me."

"*Funtington, December* 11*th*, 1878.—As it is now
some time since I heard from you, I am desirous of
knowing how your health holds out. Well, I sincerely
hope, or else you will not be able to enjoy the approaching festival. 1878 has deprived me of many
friends, and good Doctor Quin's loss is a great sorrow
for us, particularly to my afflicted wife, who, thank
God, is certainly better since our last trip to Malvern."

"*Funtington, June* 2*nd*, 1879.—We are much
grieved, my dear friend, to hear of your being pros-
trated by bronchitis, but sincerely hope that before
long you will be again all right. Broke's case was
thought to be fatal, I heard, but copious bleeding from
the wound (like his poor father's) has so far saved
him. The other side of the picture is pleasing, viz.,
the good squire's convalescence. How kind of you,
my good friend, to think of others when so afflicted,
by remembering bygone days. Alas! I believe that I
am the only one alive of the dear old *Shannons* to
receive your blessing, but I am sure all those who
have departed have your prayers for forgiveness of

sins, and for a glorious resurrection. As you have mentioned seeing my name at the First Lord's Dinner on the Queen's birthday, I will tell you that I was repaid for going by the very cordial reception I met with, and also by the kindly greeting of a few old friends. I afterwards attended Lady Salisbury's At Home, and on Monday the Levee. I therefore now think I have finished (at eighty-eight) *my public duty*, and if permitted to remain here a little longer, may my chief thoughts be employed in asking pardon and forgiveness for all my transgressions of that great God whose mercy endures for ever."

" *Funtington, June* 10*th,* 1879.—When I was in London I did not venture upon many gay doings—the First Lord's Dinner, Lady Salisbury's Soiree, and the Prince's Levee were all. I was told *H.M.S. Pinafore* was having a great run, but from what you have told me I do not regret my want of curiosity."

" *Great Malvern, August* 1879.—I regret, exceedingly, the state of the good 'squire's health. *Entre nous,* I have not written to him saying I was here, because I have not felt equal to journeying to Worcester, being sadly troubled with crippled feet, therefore have not been in a mood to ask him to let me know when he was likely to be there, and as he is unwell, it turns out all right. Your account of *H.M.S. Pinafore* makes me long to see it, and as you are fond of the music, I wish you joy at having some of her crew at Brome. What a sad summer we have had! But all must rejoice that we can get our bread and other stuffs from abroad. Malvern is now overflowing with visitors, and by comparison with other places, it seems that we have been highly favoured during the tremendous downpours. Are you not pleased to find that poor Carey has not been sacrificed to cruel party spirit? The Government are to blame for having sanctioned the Prince's going to the Cape under their wing, which has been the cause of all that followed."

"*Great Malvern, September 23rd,* 1879.—I have been anticipating until now the pleasure of another gossip with you, but ' *L'homme propose, Dieu dispose,*' and circumstances have recalled us home sooner than we expected. Since I last wrote to you I have had a trip into Cheshire, as I was anxious to see my daughter, Mrs. Perryn, of Trafford, who has been a great invalid for the last few years—not able to get down stairs since last February. But I must be thankful to the Almighty for granting her most earthly comforts, though it has pleased Him to withdraw the greatest of all blessings."

"*Funtington, December 23rd,* 1879.—I much fear that Ireland is again in a feverish state, but, in short, the whole world seems in a flame, and God only knows the sequel. What a magnificent person our good friend the squire is! All honour to him, and when you visit Worcestershire I hope you will find him in improved health. When you happen to see Broke remember me kindly to him. I think you will not regret having discarded the razor."

"*Funtington, March 4th,* 1880.—It is a long while, my dear friend, since we have exchanged a line, but I have been intending to do so for some days, to ask how you have passed through our late terrible winter. As to myself, I have been much annoyed by rheumatic gout in my right arm, and very tender feet, so much so that I kept my bed the best part of most days; but at my great age, I must expect to suffer more or less. Happily we are now on the eve of spring, so I hope by God's providence to get better; if not, His will be done. My dear wife is much better, so we are thinking of getting to Malvern some time in May, provided our old quarters are vacant at that time."

"*Funtington, May 15th,* 1880.—The weather has not been very genial. When will it be so again? Last year we had but little sunshine, and much rain— now we should be glad if the east wind would cease, and some warm rain descend. The 'times,' as well as the weather, are out of joint, and a gloomy prospect's before us. Ireland in a state of combustion, and a *Roman* sent to govern India, a man who has already sacrificed the interest of his country by the 'Treaty of Washington,' but who could not prevail upon our chief justice to add his name to such an unjust Act. However, Gladstone made him a marquis, and when he has accomplished more mischief, a duke's coronet will be placed upon his head. Oh! that we had a Bismarck as our chief, to guide us through the Straits of Scylla and Charybdis. I am glad Oxford has sent Harcourt to seek his fortune."

"*Funtington, October 21st,* 1880.—I will now thank you for your kind inquiries, and tell you we reached home safely on August 31st, after a pleasant stay at Malvern for three months, and are now once more moored at this secluded place, and glad enough to be in snug winter quarters, protected from the northerly blasts by the southdowns, and south-westerly gales by a stately row of chesnut trees ; but I regret to add, we are compelled to live in a state of seclusion, in consequence of my dear wife's extremely delicate health ; but, my dear friend, it does not fall to the lot of humanity to have all things good, but as in duty bound submit with patience to the decrees of Providence. Whilst at Malvern I was much tormented with the gout in my hands, which to this day I am not free from. You will see by the enclosed cutting,* which was sent

---

* An account of the death of James Coull, who steered the *Shannon* into action.

me by a friend, that up to the date mentioned I was
not the only *Shannon* remaining, and perhaps not
now, although I think I must be. To-day is the
anniversary of poor Nelson's death, seventy-five years
since, and well do I remember hearing of the sad
event, when in the *Cambrian* frigate in the West
Indies. I was then a middy of fourteen. I will not
touch upon the events of the present day—you have
them daily before you, and horrid ones they are.
The case of unhappy Ireland is deplorable, and I feel
for your anxiety, praying at the same time that the
Almighty will avert the apparently coming hurricane."

" *Funtington, November* 30*th*, 1880.—Pray make
whatever use you think proper of any communication
you have received from me of *Shannon's* affair. It
is, I believe, quite true that I am now the last one
of her crew living, and should the Almighty spare me
until April 12th next, I shall be ninety years old."

" *Great Malvern, August* 1*st*, 1881.—My dear
Brighton, I wish you would drop the ' Sir Provo '
when you write to me. You will observe that I have
set you the example. What you say respecting
carrying a *ball* * about you I can also verify, for a
friend of mine, the late Admiral Ryder Burton, did

---

* A ball received in action, which, becoming encuisted, gives little
further trouble.

for a number of years. As to politics, they are truly
disgusting, and as to the ' Irish Land Bill ' I will only
say *nous verrons.* We shall be here, I think, for
about another month, as my dear wife is so much
better for the kind attention of Dr. Fernie, of whom
I cannot speak too highly."

" *Great Malvern, August* 15*th*, 1881.—Have you
happened to look into Percy Fitzgerald's ' Life of
George IV.'? If so, you may have noticed, where
he relates occurrences at Queen Caroline's funeral,
' Sir Robert Wilson was dismissed the army for using
unbecoming language to the soldiers.' But he
omitted to add a note that Sir R. was reinstated, which
caused me to write and point out to him the propriety
of his doing so in his second edition. I enclose his
reply. Sir Robert Wilson's words were : ' Soldiers of
Waterloo, don't fire upon the people ; you can afford
a few stones thrown at you.' However, this was
sufficient for the king to punish any one he could
who espoused the queen's cause, and he used his
prerogative by ordering Sir R.'s name to be erased
from the army. Brougham, Hume, and others, were
not within his power, but the king never forgave
them. We have (as we generally do) enjoyed the
quietness of this place, and its perfect air, beautiful
scenery, etc., much, which with a landlord and his
wife who do their utmost to make us comfortable,
are things in this world not generally met with."

"*Funtington, April 25th*, 1882.—I write a few lines (and fear it can only be a few) from my bed, to which I have now been confined for upwards of a month by one of the severest attacks of gout yet inflicted, but was indeed gratified with (as I always am) your kind letter, upon which I wish I had the power to make my remarks ; but God's will must be done, and as I have received so many blessings from Him I must bear with patience ' His decree.' "

"*Great Malvern, June 19th*, 1882.—As to Ireland, it is high time to proclaim martial law in that unhappy country ; which, owing to having been misgoverned, has drifted into anarchy. As you are about to visit these parts, and having mentioned your intention of coming to Malvern to see me, may I beg of you not to throw away a day out of the few you may have to spare in Worcestershire ; for happy as I should be to see you (which I am sure you cannot doubt), I really think ' *le jeu ne vaut pas la chandelle* ' which only permits ' how do you do ? ' and ' good-bye ! ' I am, thank God, feeling a good deal better for the delicious air of Malvern."

"*Funtington, December 11th*, 1882.—I enclose my last letter from Admiral Preble.* I had destroyed his previous ones, and sent the pamphlet to my

* U.S. Navy.

daughter in Cheshire. There was nothing to dis
approve of in it. He seems a liberal-minded mar
We had a bountiful harvest but no apples ; the hurri
cane at blooming time, and the saline air, destroye
the prospect of a fine crop : trees and hedges looke
like having passed through a fire, and I fear many c
them will not recover from a blast not previousl;
known by the present generation. I am happy to say
so far, we have escaped the dreadful snowstorm
reported to have fallen in various parts, and hav
only as yet had a little ; but we, I conclude, wil
have neighbours' fare and an old-fashioned Christmas
which is now near at hand, so I will take this oppor
tunity of sending our best wishes that you may enjo;
a very happy one, which may God grant to all Hi
poor people. Should you see Broke, or write to him
remember us to him. And now, my dear Brighton
as Jack Frost is nibbling at my fingers' end, I mus
say God bless you, and that I am, as ever, your
sincere friend, PROVO WALLIS."

" *Great Malvern, June* 11*th,* 1883.—On Tuesday
last I posted a card to inform you of our safe arrival
at our much-prized summer quarters, without any *con-
tretemps.* The country just now is perfectly lovely,
and I was glad to hear from you such a flourishing
account of Norfolk, a county in which I have passed
many a happy day. A thousand thanks, my dear
Brighton, for your letter of May 30th, intended for

June 1st. Seventy years have now indeed passed for ever away, and I pray to the Almighty that it may not prove better that I should have been numbered with the slain on June 1st, 1813. *Apropos*, on the very anniversary I received a letter from the American Admiral Preble, congratulating me on having survived seventy years since that memorable day ; and, as you have always shown so much interest in the affair, I enclose it."

" *Funtington, Christmas Day,* 1883.—Many, many happy returns of the day. May you be in the enjoyment of perfect health, which is the greatest of earthly blessings. I am as well—indeed better than I could expect at my very great age. I recently sent you a Sussex paper, and marked an account of how nearly our magnificent cathedral spire was destroyed. It would have been a grievous misfortune had it been the case, as it was only restored about twenty years since, at a cost of between £40,000 and £50,000."

" *Funtington, February 8th,* 1884.—Thanks for sending me the Worcester paper. Poor Mr. Laslett ! * Let us hope he is happy. With respect to Lawrence's flag—a captain does not carry a distinguishing one. I conclude they mean an ensign of hers,† but how

---

* Our mutual friend, Mr. Laslett, died some days previously.

† The *Chesapeake*.

it got to Howick is unknown to me ; neither do I know whether he was buried in one. However, I know that after the poor fellow's death he was wrapped in one of the three she flew ; so, in all probability, when they placed him in his coffin it acted as his shroud, which was made by his own people. This is likely, for I recollect some verses which at that time were going the rounds, viz. :

> ' Brave Lawrence, famed for other deeds,
> Now in his country's colours bleeds.' "

" *Funtington, November* 20*th*, 1884.—As with you, all my news is gleaned ·from the daily papers, therefore I will not trouble you with a repetition. Owing to my dear wife's confirmed ill-health, and my age, we live quite a retired life. Nevertheless, my masters at the Admiralty keep me on the active list, which they tell me is a mark of honour, but took from me the one I considered the greatest, viz.: Vice-Admiral of the United Kingdom, because they did not allow it to be held by an Admiral of the Fleet. We have lately had a return visit from the Prince and Princess of Battenberg, who have taken a residence called Sennicotts, near Chichester. The Prince seems to be a jolly and manly-looking fellow, and his fair-one a nice, and I may say a pretty person ; certainly an agreeable one. I hope Broke-Middleton and his wife are well, and that the former is not feeling any ill-effects from his serious accident."

" *Funtington, New Year's Day*, 1885.—Many, many happy returns of New Year's day to you. I cannot expect any, but God may be so kind as still to add to my large number (94). It gave me great pleasure to hear of your being in such good health. Long may it continue, to enable you to do your much required work of 'turning the hearts of the disobedient,' so much wanted; yours is an enviable task, which I feel you will do well. We are living in very anxious days, and God only knows how things are to end. It seems to me that England is to be punished for her many backslidings; but I will not preach to you, but bear in mind the text I once had the pleasure to hear from your lips, ' Fret not thyself.' "

" *Funtington, March* 13*th*, 1886.—I feel sure you have attributed my long silence to the very severe weather we have had, and which seems reluctant to depart; but I cannot remain any longer without scribbling a few lines to let you know that it has pleased God to spare me, and should He do so until the 12th of next month, I shall then have completed my ninety-fifth year. That will be a long lease, and all I can say is that I feel sorry for not having made better use of the time. On the other hand, I am comforted by believing I am in the hands of a merciful Father. Excuse a short yarn, for I write from my bed, which I have occupied since the first week in

January, not being able to get about owing to rheumatic gout."

" *Funtington, May* 1*st,* 1886.—I can scarcely believe that ninety-five years have passed over my head since my appearance in this world of sorrow, but the hope of a better is our solace. What a splendid week the holidays had, which, as the papers remark, was worth waiting for. So I hope Norfolk was not an exception to the glorious sunshine. I, like the snails, crept out of my shell; and I hope your good nurse, Miss Frazer, and yourself have also enjoyed the bounty of heaven. Alas! there is, I fear, much tribulation in store for poor old England. The fate of nations seems too near, and symptoms are in view."

" *Funtington, May* 29*th,* 1886.—It indeed is seventy-three years ago since I was cruising in the good ship *Shannon,* then a young and thoughtless lieutenant, but now a worn-out sheer hulk, the fate of *all* who are permitted to arrive at my time of life, and of the majority long before. It is with much regret, my dear Brighton, that we have made up our minds to forgo the very great pleasure of visiting Malvern this season (and, as far as I am concerned, no doubt *for ever*), but prudence whispers *don't.* Well, it must be so, and I am very grateful for having been allowed to do so for thirty-two years, minus two when I was at Rio. Our late landlord and his wife will miss us, as the enclosed note will tell you. I will conclude by thanking you for telling me that you should drink my health on June 1st. May you see many more anniversaries. I cannot expect to be spared to see any. ·However,—

> ' As through this gloomy vale of life we run,
> Great Cause of all effects,—Thy will be done.' "

"*Funtington, July 3rd*, 1886.—Just a line, my dear friend Brighton, to tell you that it seems likely, by the goodness of Providence, that I shall once more have the pleasure of seeing Malvern, the late fine weather having done wonders for me, and, should I have no relapse, we think of leaving home on Tuesday the 13th prox."

Malvern, July 13th, 1886.—A post-card from Sir Provo that he had arrived.

"*Funtington, April 27th*, 1887.—I am now upon the threshold of eternity—an awful position, which can only be borne in happiness by those who put their trust in the entire mercy of God. I shall no more visit sweet Malvern, or London, both of which I thought (not long since) it possible I might accomplish. It is with regret that I have refused the First Lord's invitation to dinner, to celebrate Her Majesty's birthday (being also her jubilee), as I am now the senior officer in her navy, and have been so for upwards of two years. I have a good deal of rheumatic gout at present, but have been for a year without a red-hot fit. My wife, I am happy to say, has gone through the winter fairly well, but the extraordinary weather has been very trying to all. The only way I found to be at all comfortable, was by keeping quietly in *Blanket Bay*, under *Cape Rug*, until dinner time. And now, dear and valued friend, I cannot do better than finish with part of the soul-stirring words of ' Auld Lang Syne,' so—

> ' Here's my hand, my trusty friend.' "

" *Funtington, August 27th,* 1887.—I am getting rapidly into the ' sere and yellow leaf.' However, I will not trouble you with my ails and aches, but assure you that I endeavour to bear all my Heavenly Father's decrees with humble submission, gratefully thanking Him for the numberless blessings which I have received throughout my days."

" *Funtington, March 5th,* 1888.—I make an effort to let you know that I am still in the land of the living, as you may have some doubts upon the subject. The truth is, my dear friend, I have throughout the very severe winter we have experienced been obliged to keep my bed (from which I now write), tormented with rheumatic gout and other ills, smarting under the weight of extreme old age ; but when the weather

settles to snail and butterfly days, I may be permitted
to once more write you more freely."

" *Funtington, June 1st,* 1888.—My sincere and
best thanks for your affectionate letter in anticipation
of to-day, but hearing of your attack by the painful
malady, gout, caused me much sorrow.   You have my
deep sympathy.   As for myself, I am a very poor,
worn-out old creature, and of course cannot expect to
be anything else whilst it may please God to let me
remain on earth.

> ' But hush, my soul, nor dare repine,
>   The time my God appoints is best ;
> Whilst here to do His will be mine,
>   And His to fix my time of rest.'

We have been severely afflicted.   My wife's maid has
been nearly dead, and our upper housemaid died suddenly.   Our departed maid lived with us forty-two
years."

" *Funtington, September 7th,* 1888.—I had hoped
when the summer came that I might have been able
to leave my bed, but have been obliged to keep sheltered in ' Blanket Bay,' and have nearly read my eyes
out by spelling the *Times* and *Globe*.   I will send you
a letter (in answer to mine) from Sir Thomas Symonds,
a fine chip of the old sailor, and whose letters I daresay
you have read in the papers."

" *Funtington, September* 14*th*, 1888.—I write you just a line, for writing has become a task, to tell you that I was agreeably surprised last Saturday by a call from Lady Broke-Middleton."

" *Funtington, February* 27*th*, 1889.—It seems, my dear B., that you have not received a memo. card which I posted you last week (20th), but as I have been reading of so many defaults of postmen lately, no doubt it has been tampered with. Many thanks, my valued friend, for your constant wish to know how I am going on. I am, as this scrawl will tell you, up to date in the land of the living, and I wish I could say free from the infirmities of old age. I read in the paper the death of Dunsany,* and, from what you tell me of his character, he is no doubt happy."

" *Funtington, April* 17*th*, 1889.—I received with gratitude your valued birthday thoughts of me, and hope you will forgive my tardy reply; but I have really had so many letters to answer, that they who are my real friends, and you stand foremost, will make allowance. I still keep my bed; how much longer, God only knows."

---

* Admiral Lord Dunsany.

"*Funtington, May* 18*th*, 1889.—As I am now, like a snail—owing to fine weather—out of my shell, I take the opportunity of thanking you for your kind letter. As to the 1st of June to which you allude, it will not bring any pleasure to me. I long have ceased from worldly doings to feel any comfort. I know that all here is but vanity and vexation of spirit :—

> ' Our days are like the grass,
> Or as the morning flower ;
> If one sharp blast sweep o'er the field
> It withers in an hour.
> But Thy compassions, Lord,
> To endless years endure,
> And children's children ever find
> Thy words of promise sure.' "

"*Funtington, July* 18*th*, 1889.—I remain much the same. St. Swithin's rain has done much good, if the good saint will but be moderate."

"*Funtington, October* 4*th*, 1889.—I have not been quite the thing for the last week, which will account for my tardy reply to your last. Alas ! my beloved friend, I am becoming weaker and weaker. My wonder is that I am still alive ; but I will say no more on this subject, as you are in possession of my thoughts. Of course you have my full permission to do as you intend respecting the Biography."

" *Funtington, January 16th,* 1890.—The death
of my daughter, Mrs. Perryn, of Trafford Hall, near
Chester, which occurred on the second of this month,
has been a severe blow to me. It was quite sudden,
or nearly so. She fell down in her bedroom, and
expired in twenty-four hours. This sad event has
heaped such severe sorrow upon me that I scarcely
know what I am about. I can write no more, but
only subscribe myself, as ever, most affectionately
and sincerely yours, P. W. P. WALLIS."

Fentiman
April 18th 1891

My beloved Brighton

I wish I could write you a letter, but alas I am quite hors-de-combat but you have my heart's best wishes, and this is perhaps the last time I shall be able to write to you so I can only say, may our heavenly Father have you in his holy keeping. Give my kind regards to Miss Fraser I can no more, my good Butts will send you a paper now and then. Once more God bless you, prays your sincere friend

J. W. Wallis.

FACSIMILE OF THE LAST LETTER WRITTEN BY SIR PROVO TO DR. BRIGHTON.

XI.

AT FUNTINGTON.

CHAPTER X.

AT FUNTINGTON.

NEAR the dividing line of Hampshire and Sussex, and in the south-western corner of the last-mentioned county, lies the little village of Funtington, one of the many old-fashioned and picturesque villages that may be found along the border-land of these two counties. It has not yet been wakened from its quietude by the whistle of the railway-engine, nor is its tranquillity much disturbed by vehicular traffic, for there is no main road running through it. Hidden by surrounding woods and its own stately elms, it escapes observation; and being not too easily accessible, is not much sought by excursionists, though an occasional tourist will pass that way—more especially, perhaps, to catch a glimpse of Funtington House, where Sir Provo has spent a long and happy life of retirement. From Chichester, more than elsewhere, come the visitors

14

to Funtington, not only because it is the nearest place of importance, but more especially because in that old Roman city, with its twelfth-century cathedral and Tudor market-cross, there reside many of England's naval heroes and veterans of the sea, ending their days in peace within easy reach of the ocean on which they have spent the greater part of their lives, and convenient to the great naval station of Portsmouth, which they know so well.

The distance from Chichester to Funtington is not great—only some six miles—and in summer time, when the firs, oaks, and beeches of the "Old Broyle" are in full leaf, the drive is altogether pleasant; but if a short walk be preferred, Funtington can be reached by pretty lanes or across the fields, in a leisurely walk of something less than an hour, from the old-world village of Bosham, to which a train from Chichester will carry you in a few minutes. But you might well stay a little at Bosham, if only to look at its fine Saxon church, which not only contains the remains of Canute's daughter, and the secretary of Thomas à Becket, but also makes a conspicuous feature in the Bayeux tapestry, for it was from the harbour of Bosham, or "Bosenham," that Harold sailed on his voyage to Normandy, the site of his residence being still pointed out.

Funtington is rich in trees, and Funtington House owes some of its seclusion to them, but more to the high wall which partly surrounds it, and which for some distance marks the boundary of the road. Entering by a simple carriage gateway, the pillars of which are surmounted by two stone cannon balls, you are at once struck by the well-kept state of the grounds. The lawn is trimly cut and refreshingly green; the beds are in good order; the laurels bordering the lawn closely set and well grown, making a solid background, and successfully hiding the coarser part of the garden.

The house is unpretentious though roomy, is old-fashioned in appearance, and is, in fact, old; but you will be told at Funtington that water has never yet been known to leak through the roof, old as it is. Much else that is about you is old—the trees, the ivy, the evergreens, and the moss and lichen-covered wall; and within the house is the brave old Admiral himself, who, since he came here, after his last voyage in the *Cumberland*, in 1858, has added thirty-three years to his life.

Inside, the house is warm and snug. The hall, which you will reach in less than twenty paces from the entrance to the grounds, is neither large nor lofty, but there is room for many interesting trophies, curios and works of art. It is spanned midway by an arch, above which is an array of swords, spears, and weapons of other kinds, some of which have been brought by the Admiral at different times from foreign parts, while others have been acquired at home. The sword presented to him by his old captain of the

Shannon has the place of honour, whilst that of a King of Naples hangs close by. Interspersed with these are some rare pipe-stems and silver head-gear, and right in front of you, at the end of the hall, is a fine white marble bust of Napoleon I., supported by a stone pedestal, the base of which is covered with bees, in brass, and other Imperial emblems.

The walls of the hall are covered with paintings and engravings, nearly all of which are in one way or another connected with our naval history. Two sea-pieces by Musin occupy a considerable space, and around them are a number of smaller pictures, several depicting the scenes which arose out of the famous action of the *Shannon* and the *Chesapeake*, whilst another shows the *Cleopatra* struggling with her far more powerful antagonist the *Ville de Milan*. But beneath these pictures of storm and war you may see a handsome table, inlaid in coloured marbles, with the peaceful design of pigeons feeding from a bowl, and all around you are specimens of art in Oriental china and other ware, there being in one corner an old cabinet quite full of it.

Turning round, you are met with quite a number of engraved portraits of well-known men, among them being George IV. when Prince of Wales, and his brother, the Duke of York. These two engravings were presented to Sir Provo's grandfather, William Lawlor, by the father of Queen Victoria, H.R.H. Edward, Duke of Kent, when Commander-in-chief of His Majesty's forces in Nova Scotia, a portrait of the Duke himself, which Sir Provo keeps by him in his bedroom, having been presented at the same time.

Other interesting portraits are those of Lord Nelson, Captain Broke, and Lady Wallis's father, the late General Sir Robert Wilson. It will have been seen how, quite undeservedly as Sir Provo says, Sir Robert got into disgrace with George IV., and was dismissed the army, to be, however, afterwards reinstated. To commemorate this event, a picture was painted representing the present Lady Wallis in the act of restoring to her father's hat the plumes of which it had been deprived. Sir Provo took a great interest in helping to clear Sir Robert's name from the stigma cast upon it, and it was owing to him that some of the incidents recorded in the life of Sir Robert, which was edited by Sir Provo's brother-in-law, the Rev. Herbert Randolph, are preserved.

In the study to the left of the hall you will find, among many volumes of naval history, a case of books on Egypt given to Sir Robert Wilson by General Count Lavalette, whose life Sir Robert once saved ; a snuff-box made from a fragment of the bold *Chesapeake* adorns the mantel-shelf, and about you are other little memorials of the famous fight. Here, amidst the records of gallant deeds, in some of which he has himself taken part, Sir Provo has passed many a pleasant hour inditing letters on those closing scenes of the Long War with America which he could so well describe from his own intimate knowledge, and as to which his recollections have been frequently requested from both sides of the Atlantic. Indeed, when the American naval authorities were preparing a history of the war many years since, that portion which relates to the action of the *Shannon* and *Chesapeake* was submitted by them to Sir Provo for amendment.

Crossing the hall, you take a peep into the drawing-room to look at the miniature of Sir Ralph Abercrombie, and then pass into the adjoining dining-room, through the French windows of which can be seen the old English garden, a magnificent evergreen oak rising from the lawn directly in front, and reaching as high as the house itself. Everything is quiet and tranquil, and as you look out into the distance your thoughts are inclined to wander back to the hall pictures and the events of the long-gone June 1st, 1813, and somewhat reluctantly return to the objects immediately near.

The first that attracts your attention is a portrait hanging between the two windows, which is so strikingly like that you have seen of Sir Provo at the age of twenty-two, and which hangs in Lady Wallis's own room, that you venture to suggest it is a copy, but are informed that it is a portrait of Sir Provo's father when a young man. On comparing the two pictures you will find a difference in the pose of the head, otherwise the likeness is remarkable.

On the larger walls are some big cattle pieces, and two village scenes; in a niche over the sideboard a cast of the face of Charles XII. of Sweden, taken after his death, and on the sideboard itself a piece of plate presented to Sir Provo by the Council of Foreign Bondholders, of which he was one of the original founders. Taking a glance up the stairs you find, looking benignly down upon you, a large portrait of Admiral Lord Howe, whose famous victory over the French fleet in 1795—the year when Sir Provo was first entered on a ship's books—was also gained on the 1st of June, a date which was to be made more glorious by the victory of the *Shannon.*

As you pass out into the delightful garden, you cannot help thinking how well the grounds harmonise with the house. The elms with their ivy-covered trunks, the stately chesnuts, the beds stocked with old English flowers, the tall hawthorns and evergreens, the creeper-covered porch, and sturdy fruit trees clinging to the old wall, all give token of age. Not far off are the roofs of a few cottages and farm buildings, and the pasture land on which Sir Provo's cattle are grazing, for he has taken an interest in small farming, and Funtington House claims some acres of ground. You may also see the two ponds, now united, but still not large, on which Sir Provo, in quite his old age, took gentle exercise and pleasure in pulling his boat with his wife as a companion, to finish with a sailor's lunch after his exertions; and also the little spring or fountain from which the village takes its name of Fountain Town or Funtington, though it has never yet become a town.

In this secluded spot, where all his surroundings speak of age, Sir Provo has passed in peaceful quietude the long eventide of his life, growing older and older, but retaining until quite recently plenty of freshness and vigour. Year by year he migrated to the far-distant town of Malvern, which to him was a second home, until the year 1886, when in the ninety-sixth year of his age, his last visit was made. Small surprise then that his brother Admiral of the Fleet, Sir Thomas Symonds, should call him not only a "dear old naval giant," but "a wonder of the world."

There have not been many visitors to Funtington House for some years, but one among the few visits paid was that of Prince and Princess Louis of Battenberg, who greatly pleased Sir Provo with a call from their adjacent house of Sennicotts.

Sir Provo has not lacked occupation for his leisure hours. He was able to read easily until within the last year or so, and made good use of his power in going again over his naval histories and the life and private journal of his father-in-law, and in closely following the news contained in the *Times* and the *Globe*, which even now he insists on having read to him by his butler, who finds that the veteran Admiral is not slow to criticise and to express strong opinions on subjects which are interesting to him, and especially when naval matters are in question. His memory keeps marvellously clear, and he frequently recalls incidents of his early days, and can detail with great accuracy the circumstances connected with the exploits in which he had a share.

Many there are who will prize letters written by the Admiral after he had passed his ninetieth year, for he has always been ready to answer in a kindly way the various questions that have been put to him by Americans as well as Englishmen regarding the famous action, and to set right those who have now and then stumbled into error in their descriptions. Naval men of both countries have from time to time, and particularly on the anniversaries of the action and Sir Provo's birthday, sent him their congratulations by telegram and post, and frequent communications have been addressed to him on matters which the writers have thought would be interesting. In later days, when the number of these communications increased, and the Admiral was less able to write, he could only be grateful for the kindly interest taken in him, and could not acknowledge his thanks as he would have wished.

Among those who corresponded with Sir Provo

was Admiral Preble, two of whose kindly letters, coming as they do from an officer of the United States Navy, and being on subjects interesting to Sir Provo, are appended :—

"COTTAGE FARM, BROOKLINE, MASS.,
"*November 4th*, 1882.

"MY DEAR SIR,—

It gave me pleasure, about a week since, to send you a photograph of myself and of the old man about town, the last survivor of the *Chesapeake*. I will now endeavour to thank you for your letter of October 11th, and the photograph which came with it, and which I value highly. The 'Souls of Soldiery' which you mention, and which was composed of retired commissioned officers of the State Militia, no longer exists, and has been merged in a similar and much older military organisation called the 'Ancient and Honourable Artillery,' of which the Prince of Wales is an honorary member, and which has passed its 250th anniversary. It is the oldest military organisation of our new country. The General Lyman you mention was subsequently the Mayor of Boston, and has long since passed on. His son, General Theodore Lyman, is now a candidate for Congress.

"I notice one misapprehension in your letter. My great-uncle did not command the *Chesapeake* at the time of the affair of the *Leopard*. She was then com-

manded by Commodore Barron.* My uncle, Edward
Preble, of Tripolitan fame, was then sick and on
what proved his death-bed. When he heard of the
affair, he raised himself up in bed and exclaimed:
'Would to God I had been there! Would to God I
had been there!'

"The United States, by emigration from Germany,
Ireland, and elsewhere, is fast losing its Anglo-Saxon
type; but in New England, which is the parent of
Western emigration, we of the old stock are Anglo-
Saxons. I can trace my children's pedigree back in
all its branches (seven generations) to the emigrants
from old England, some of whom came over in the
Mayflower. Yet in the neighbouring city of Boston,
one-fifth at least of its inhabitants are of Irish descent
—the Biddies of our domestic service and the common
labourers being largely of Celtic origin, though an
infusion of Swedes and Germans has stepped in of
late.

"I wish you could see the Boston of to-day, with
its half a million of inhabitants, and which its

---

* It may be mentioned that the *Chesapeake*, some years before her
action with the *Shannon*, had been brought to by the *Leopard*, and
several English deserters taken from her. Her commander, Barron,
was tried by court-martial and suspended. About ten years afterwards it was proposed that he should have another command; but
Commodore Stephen Decatur, then serving as a Commissioner of the
Navy, strongly objected. This led to a fiery correspondence between
the two Commodores, resulting in a duel, fought March 22nd, 1820,
when Decatur was killed and Barron seriously wounded.—J. G. B.

denizens call ' the Hub of the Universe.' Since you
saw it, its little peninsula of 750 acres has become
some 3000 or 4000 of made land, and its narrowest
part has become—by the transportation of the gravelly
hills of the country into the city—its widest. It has
also enveloped in its government the neighbouring
towns of Charlestown, Roxbury, and Brighton. On
the new-made land are the handsomest public buildings and private residences, the widest streets, and the
finest parks and statues.

"But I am afraid I am tiring you with this long
letter and my crooked handwriting, for which I have
not the excuse of gouty fingers, and I echo your wish
and pray I may never experience them. My grandfather, however, who was brigadier-general of provincial troops, and served in the campaign of General
Wolfe, died at the close of our revolutionary war of
gout—and old age; and according to rule I ought to
inherit it from him.

"Your photographs I readily recognised through
the earlier portrait which is printed in the memoir
of Sir P. Broke. I would ask you why he did not
continue in active service. Was it from physical dis-
ability by reason of his wounds?

"It is astonishing how obstinate some people are:
an old gentleman endeavoured, the other day, to
convince me that the action between the *Chesapeake*
and *Shannon* was fought *inside Boston lights!* He
was then a boy of six or seven, and saw the action

from Milton Hill, and puts his boyish recollections of what he saw against the direct evidence of the men who were engaged in the conflict. He evidently saw the *Chesapeake* fire her challenging gun as she came down at four o'clock, as he states *that* as the time when the action commenced, and says ' *there were no broadsides fired !* ' Also that ' *it was blowing fresh,*' because ' *he saw the ships reef topsails.*' He is not only very obstinate, but very deaf, and I found it useless to try to convince him contrary to his recollections.

"It does not seem possible that England and the United States could ever drift into another war. May that day be long delayed or never happen.

"I have the honour to be,

"Very truly yours,

"Geo. Henry Preble.

"Sir Provo Wm. Parry Wallis, G.C.B., etc., etc."

"Cottage Farm Station,

"Brookline, Mass.,

"*May* 18*th*, 1883.

"Dear Admiral Wallis,—

"I write this morning a few lines, hoping they will reach you on June 1st to congratulate you on your good health on the *seventieth* anniversary of your memorable victory over the *Chesapeake*.

"The old sailor Trefethern still lives, I believe, though I have not seen or heard from him for several months. There died here recently an old woman, who was the keeper of Boston Lighthouse at the time of the action. I have mislaid the newspaper notice of her death, or I would send it you. I sent a few days since, by mail, to your address, a copy of our Navy Register for this year, thinking perhaps among those on the retired list you might find some familiar names. I also send you to-day a copy of my review of the life of our Rear-Admiral Dahlgren, thinking it may interest you.

" We have had a cold spring, but the trees are now in leaf and blossom, and the grass on my lawn fresh and green. I must not forget to thank you for your note of April 28th, and the enclosed birth-day card. I am happy to say this leaves me and my family, consisting of a son and daughter, all in good health. I visited New York last week with my daughter to see some friends off to Europe, whose departure made me to wish I was going also. I have an old friend in your service, now on the retired list, whom you may know—Vice-Admiral Edward W. Vansittart. We hunted pirates together in China in 1854. I also knew on that station and at that time, Sir Fleetwood Pellew and Sir James Stirling (both now dead), and the latter's son, who is now, I see, a Vice-Admiral on the active list, as is also Vice-Admiral Chas. Fellowes, C.B. Sir George Sartorius I met in Lisbon in 1863, and saluted both as an English and a Portuguese Admiral.

Admiral Sir Henry Keppel I think I met in China, in 1844, in command of the *Dido,* and Admiral Sir Charles Elliot when in command of a frigate in China in 1854.

"Of the junior officers of the Royal Navy I have quite an extensive acquaintance.

"Wishing you many happy returns of the 1st of June,

  "I am,

    "Sincerely and very truly yours,

      "GEO. HENRY PREBLE.

"Sir Provo W. P. Wallis, G.C.B., Admiral of the Fleet, etc., etc."

As I shall have to devote some space to the congratulations received by the Admiral on entering the hundred and first year of his age, I will not introduce further copies of letters previously written to him on the anniversaries of the days to which I have just alluded; but I should like to mention that on the last night of their manœuvres in Bantry Bay, in 1888, on the anniversary of the capture of the *Chesapeake,* the captain and officers of the modern *Shannon* did not forget the brave and sole surviving representative of the *Shannon* of our history, but sent him a telegram of hearty goodwill. Doubtless they are proud of the name of their ship, and ready to emulate the heroic deeds of those who belonged to the old *Shannon,* should occasion require. What a comparison might be made between our old friend and the modern armoured cruiser of the same name, with her 400 or 500 men, heavy guns, and big engine-power!

On the completion of his hundredth year, on Sunday, April 12th, 1891, the newspapers—those current and valuable records of the passing day— American, British, and Nova Scotian, abounded with biographical notices of the " Father of the British Fleet," as he was universally (and with justice) designated. A song descriptive of the *Shannon's* victory was dedicated to him, and his portrait, in full uniform, with the insignia of the Bath, the medal with the three clasps—*Shannon* and *Chesapeake*, *Ans-la-Barque*, and *Guadaloupe*—which no other living man is entitled to wear, and his orders upon his breast, was painted for him and presented by the Admiral to the Royal Sailors' Home at Portsea, and is likely to become historical, Lady Wallis having approved of it as an excellent likeness. Congratulations came from all quarters of the globe in great profusion, for it may be truly said that his reputation was almost world-wide, and his name revered wherever known.

From the many letters and telegrams received by the Admiral on this memorable anniversary of his birthday, I have made the following selection, whilst regretting that want of space compels me to omit many that it would have much pleased me to insert. It will be observed that among the letters is one from Mr. Childers, of whom Sir Provo a few years ago said : "I am grateful to him for the dearest of all distinctions. It is, at any rate, a pleasant thing to know that although eighty-three years have rolled by since I donned my middy's uniform, my name will remain where it is as long as God is pleased to spare me."

TELEGRAMS.

FROM HER MAJESTY THE QUEEN.

[Handed in at the Office of H.M.'s Admiralty 9.53 a.m.]

" *To Admiral of the Fleet, Sir Provo Wallis, G.C.B.*

"The following telegram has been received from General Sir Henry Ponsonby, Grasse, France :—

" 'I congratulate you on your hundredth birthday.'

" ' V.R.I.' "

FROM HIS ROYAL HIGHNESS THE PRINCE OF WALES.

[Handed in at the Sandringham Office 7.33 m.]

" *To Admiral of the Fleet, Sir Provo Wallis, G.C.B., Funtington, Chichester.*

"The Prince of Wales congratulates the senior Admiral of the Fleet on his having attained the one hundredth anniversary of his birthday, and wishes him health and happiness."

15

FROM HIS ROYAL HIGHNESS THE DUKE OF CAMBRIDGE.

[Handed in at West Strand Office at 3.24 m.]

" To Admiral of the Fleet, Sir P. Wallis,
Funtington, Chichester.

" As Commander-in-Chief of the Army I congratulate you on your hundredth anniversary of your birthday.

"CAMBRIDGE."

" To Admiral of the Fleet, Sir Provo Wallis,
Funtington, Chichester.

"Best congratulations to the centenarian Admiral of the Fleet, from the Admiral and officers of the German Squadron, now in Plymouth Sound.

"ADMIRAL SCHRÖEDER."

.

[Handed in at the Halifax (Nova Scotia) Office.]

" To Admiral Sir Provo Wallis, Chichester, Sussex.

" The Mayor and Corporation of Halifax, on behalf of the citizens, offer to Admiral Sir Provo Wallis their cordial congratulations on his reaching his one hundredth birthday, and assure him that his distinguished services are remembered with pride in his native city.

"DAVID McPHERSON, *Mayor.*"

" *To Admiral Sir P. Wallis, Funtington House,
Chichester.*

" Beg to render my very sincere congratulations on
your attaining your hundredth birthday, and shall
hope you may be spared to see several more.

" Captain W. Sarbly."

" *To Sir Provo Wallis, Funtington, Sussex, England.*

" Captain and officers H.M.S. *Victoria* send you
their best wishes on your hundredth birthday."

[Handed in at the Simmonstown Office, at 9 a.m.]

" *To Sir Provo Wallis, Chichester.*

" Hearty congratulations—Admiral, Captain and
officers, *Raleigh.*"

[Handed in at the Devonport Office, at 6.5 p.m.]

" *To Admiral Sir Provo Wallis, Funtington House,
near Chichester.*

" Captain and officers H.M.S. *Shannon* heartily
congratulate Admiral Sir Provo Wallis on attaining
his centenary, and wish him many happy returns of
the day."

" *To Admiral of the Fleet, Sir Provo W. P. Wallis,
Funtington, Chichester.*

" The Committee of the Royal Navy Club, now
sitting, offer hearty congratulations on your having

attained the one hundredth anniversary of your birthday, and seventy-fifth of your membership of Club.

"KELLY."

"*To Admiral of the Fleet, Sir Provo Wallis, G.C.B.*

"Hearty congratulations on attaining your one hundredth birthday, from Dr. Henry Smith, son of your old *Shannon* shipmate, Captain W. Smith.

"*To Admiral of the Fleet, Sir Provo Wallis, Funtington, near Bosham.*

"Warmest congratulations and kindest regards to Lady Wallis and yourself.

"Dr. MARTIN (Portsmouth)."

"*To Admiral Sir Provo Wallis, Funtington, Chichester.*

"Accept sincere congratulations on entering into your hundred and first year.

"GUEDALLA, GRESHAM CLUB, London."

LETTERS.

FROM HIS ROYAL HIGHNESS THE DUKE OF EDINBURGH.

"ADMIRALTY HOUSE, MOUNT WISE, DEVONPORT,
"*April* 16*th*, 1891.

"MY DEAR SIR PROVO WALLIS,—

"For months past I have been bearing in mind the approach of the historic event of your entering upon your one hundred and first year of age. The hunt we were all on, upon the day itself, owing to the arrival of a German Squadron, caused me to overlook it until after the telegraph offices were closed, it being Sunday.

"I should be very sorry to think that you should consider me unmindful on so memorable an occasion, and now beg you to accept my warmest congratulations, although they arrive too late. I trust at the same time that we may still long be able to count you as our senior Admiral of the Fleet.

"The ship which bears the celebrated name of the one in which you served as second lieutenant during her celebrated action, is now in port here, and recalls to all present the part you took on that occasion.

"Believe me, yours very truly,

"ALFRED."

FROM PRINCE LOUIS OF BATTENBERG.

"H.M.S. *Scout*, PLATEI, GREECE, *April 8th*, 1891.

"MY DEAR ADMIRAL,—

"Will you allow me, as a naval officer and a former neighbour of yours in Sussex, to join my most heartfelt congratulations to those of thousands of others on the occasion of your completing your hundredth year. Were I not serving on a foreign station, I should most certainly have gone to Funtington to wish you joy in person, and I look forward on my return to England to renewing our acquaintance. My wife, whom you will, I dare say, remember, joins most heartily in my congratulations. I only left her a few days ago at Malta. She particularly charged me to remember her to you very kindly.

"Begging you to present my respects to Lady Wallis, .

"I remain, yours most sincerely and obediently,

"LOUIS BATTENBERG,

"Commander R.N., Commanding H.M.'s Ship *Scout*."

"*April 21st*, 1891.

" MY DEAR SIR PROVO WALLIS,—

"I hope that you will allow me to offer you my sincere congratulations on your hundredth birthday. I knew that you were born in 1791, but I was not aware of the actual day till I read a notice of the celebration of your centenary in the newspapers. It has been a great satisfaction to me to have been the instrument of retaining on the flag list the name of the first Admiral in history who has reached the age of one hundred, and I hope that you may see a good many more birthdays.

"I am not quite sure about your address, but I hope that this will reach you.

"Believe me to be, yours very sincerely,

"HUGH CHILDERS."

" Southampton Dock Company, *April 9th,* 1891.

" To Admiral of the Fleet, Sir Provo William Parry Wallis, G.C.B.

" We, the undersigned, who for many years were associated with you in the conduct of the affairs of the Southampton Dock Company, are desirous of availing ourselves of this opportunity, marking as does the centenary epoch of an honoured life, to present our congratulations on the event, and of recording the homage of our esteem and regard for one whose distinguished career throughout a stainless life so eminently deserves.

" Stewart Macnaghten, *Chairman.*
Ed. Morris, *Deputy Chairman.*
Fred. H. Kerr, *Director.*
Thomas H. M. Martin, ,,
G. Colvile,   ,,
Ralph Dutton,   ,,
Hy. Campill,   ,,
M. Portal,   ,,
Jas. Gilbert Johnston, ,,
Percy Mortimer,   ,,
Frank H. Evans,   ,,
C. Hemery,   ,,
     Philip Hedges, *Secretary.*"

"Council of Foreign Bondholders,
"17, Moorgate Street, London,
"*April* 18*th,* 1891.

" *Admiral of the Fleet, Sir Provo Wallis, G.C.B.,*
Funtington House, near Chichester.

"Dear Sir,—

"I am desired by the Council of the Corporation of Foreign Bondholders to convey to you their congratulations on the occasion of the centenary of your birth.

"They cannot allow this happy event to pass without expressing to you their admiration of the great services you have rendered your country during your long and distinguished career, and also their sincere appreciation of the high honour done to this Institution by your connection with it, which they are proud to think dates from its foundation, and which they venture to hope may yet be continued for many years to come.

"I remain, Dear Sir, yours truly,
"C. O'Leary, *Secretary.*"

I may add that among the tributes called forth by this interesting event was the following sonnet from the pen of Mr. Theodore Watts, which appeared in the *Athenæum* :—

TO NOVA SCOTIA

ON THE HUNDREDTH BIRTHDAY OF SIR PROVO WALLIS, G.C.B.,
SENIOR ADMIRAL OF THE FLEET.

England, whose far off children love to ride
　　Her subject billows, thanks thee for thy son :
　　The queen whose olden strength is but begun,
Whose right of might is still, though waxing wide,
By motherhood of nations justified,—
　　Whose robes of empire Freedom's hands have spun
　　On every loom of Ocean 'neath the sun,—
Hails thee with love this morn, and tears of pride.

" Daughter," saith she, " though many a year hath sped
　　Since that great Sunday when thy sailor led
　　The *Chesapeake* to thee—the proudest prize
　　　Fate ever won from chance by England's cannon—
　　That Sunday lends to this what never dies,
　　　The hero-hallowed light that lights the *Shannon*."

Sunday, April 12th, 1891.　　　　　　THEODORE WATTS.

That Her Majesty the Queen, then at Grasse,
France, should have thought of Sir Provo on this
occasion, touched him deeply. The letter from
H.R.H. the Duke of Edinburgh was a personal
remembrance, for Sir Provo had met the Duke at
an official dinner, when the late Mr. W. H. Smith
was the First Lord of the Admiralty, and by request
remained behind to converse with him after most
of the guests had gone.

The telegram from the mayor and corporation
of Halifax gave Sir Provo much pleasure, and he
was not a little delighted to be presented with a

Malacca cane, bearing the following inscription :
"To Admiral of the Fleet, Sir Provo W. P.
Wallis, G.C.B., on his 100th birthday, from the
granddaughter of his old friend and comrade, Sir
Philip B. V. Broke."

The venerable Admiral could in but very few
instances give special thanks for these kind attentions,
but he says he was very gratified by receiving them.
His writing is perhaps now getting almost a thing
of the past, and probably the letter of which a fac-
simile is given in this volume is the last he has
written, but I trust it will not, as he suggests, be the
last he ever will write. He is again sheltered in
"Blanket Bay" under "Cape Rug," which he will,
if spared, continue to make his winter quarters; but
when "butterfly days" come again, I hope he will be
able with them to glory in the sunshine that makes
Funtington House one of the brightest spots for many
miles round. Its owner, notwithstanding he is now
obliged to keep to his bedroom, is the same genial
man I have ever known him to be, and of whose
kindly nature I have had ample proof. He is still
able to recount the incidents of his life in an enter-
taining manner to those who are privileged to be
with him; for, notwithstanding his great age, his
memory remains wonderfully accurate and clear.

The seat of the descendant of his late
Sir Drew William Drury Wolles K C B

Page 253.

XII.

RECOLLECTIONS OF WORCESTERSHIRE.

CHAPTER XII.

I MUST now carry myself back to a time when I had not for long been personally acquainted with the Admiral, and give my recollections of a few of the many happy days spent with him at and about his favourite resort—Malvern ; where, for between thirty and forty years, he passed his autumnal holidays.

"Is it possible ? " said the Admiral, one sunny morning in June 1865, as we were strolling in front of Scarsdale Villa, his pleasant summer residence at Malvern, " Is it possible that you are a Worcestershire man ? "

" Yes, indeed, born and bred within some twelve miles of the spot where we now stand."

" Well, I have summered here for so many years, I may call myself half a Worcestershire man."

" My first recollection," said I, " carries me back to 1839, when Malvern was not half the size it now is. We drove over, a party of four, and alighted at the then Belle Vue Hotel. ' What can we have for dinner ?' I asked. ' Anything, sir.' ' Good : give us the best you can.' And bad was the best. Badly cooked mutton-cutlets, defying mastication, vegetables half done, and stale pastry. Little dinner ate we that day. No doubt the railway now supplies you amply ? "

" Yes, we have no room for complaints. We have, too, a good library, and the best medical attendance."

" Do you know much of the earlier history of Malvern ? "

" No, only since our sojourn here."

I then proceeded to give the Admiral some particulars, which I venture to repeat in the hope that, being more or less " ancient history," they will prove interesting to my readers, and more especially to those who are familiar with this lovely spot.

It was during the craze for hydropathy, more than sixty years ago, that the then little village sprang into something like notice. Pure air and the purest water, quietude, varied scenery and extensive views, constituted its attractions ; but it was reserved for poor Dr. Gully, so fatally connected with the " Bravo-Ricardo " case, to bring them more prominently into patronage.

About the time of " Queen Anne " the village of Great Malvern contained only fifty houses, and in the influx of visitors during the summer months was quite inadequate for their accommodation—so much so that the surplus visitors were lodged in tents. The physicians who were instrumental in bringing this valuable Spa to the knowledge of the public were principally Doctors Wilson, Wall, and Johnstone, of Worcester; but I am afraid their combined efforts did not equal those of the parish clerk in the unhappy days of King Charles I., who thus chanted its praises :—

"On the Malvern Wells.

"As I did walk alone,
　Late in an evening,
I heard the voice of one
　Most sweetly singing;
Which did delight me much,
Because was such,
And ended with a touch; *
　'O praise the Lord!'

"The God of sea and land
　That rules above us,
Stays His avenging hand,
　'Cause He doth love us,
And doth His blessings send,
Although we do offend;
Then let us all amend,
　And 'praise the Lord.'

"Great Malvern on a rock,
　Thou standest surely;
Do not thyself forget,
　Living securely.

* "Touch," a chorus or refrain.

16

Thou hast of blessing store,
No country town hath more;
Do not forget, therefore,
 To 'praise the Lord.'

"Thou hast a famous church,
 And rarely builded;
No country town hath such,
 Most men have yielded.
For pillars stout and strong,
And windows large and long,
Remember in thy song
 To 'praise the Lord.'

"There is God's service read,
 With rev'rence duly;
There is His Word preached,
 Learned and truly.
And every Sabbath day,
Singing of psalms, they say
It is surely the only way
 To 'praise the Lord.'

"The sun in glory great,
 When first it riseth,
Doth bless thy happy seat
 And thee adviseth,
That then 'tis time to pray,
That God may bless thy way,
And keep thee all the day
 To 'praise the Lord.'

"That thy prospect is good,
 None can deny thee:
Thou hast great store of wood
 Growing hard by thee,
Which is a blessing great,
To roast and boil thy meat,
And thee in cold to heat.
 O 'praise the Lord!'

" Preserve it, I advise,
    Whilst thou hast it ;
Spare not in any wise,
    But do not waste it,
Lest thou repent too late—
Remember Hanley's fate—
In time shut up thy gate
    And ' praise the Lord.'

" A chase for royal deer
    Round doth beset thee ;
Too many I doe fear
    For aught they get thee.
Yet though they eat away
Thy corn, and grass, and hay,
Doe not forget, I say,
    To ' praise the Lord.'

" That noble chase doth give
    Thy beasts their feeding,
Where they in summer live,
    With little needing.
Thy swine and sheep they go,
So doth thy horse also,
Till winter brings in snow :
    Then ' praise the Lord.'

" Turn up thine eyes on high :
    There fairly standing
See Malvern's highest hill
    All hills commanding.
They all confess at will
Their sovereign, Malvern Hill.
Let it be mighty still ;
    O ' praise the Lord.'

" When western winds doe rock
    Both town and country,
Thy hill doth break the shock ;
    They cannot hurt thee.

When waters great abound,
And many a country's drown'd,
Thou standest safe and sound.
    O ' praise the Lord.'

" Out of that famous hill
    There daily springeth
A water, passing still,
    Which always bringeth
Great comfort to all them
That are diseased men,
And makes them well again
    To ' praise the Lord.'

" Hast thou a wound to heal
    The which doth grieve thee?
Come, then, unto this well,
    It will relieve thee :
Noli me tangeres
And other maladies
Have here their remedies,
    ' Praised be the Lord.'

" To drink thy waters, store
    Lie in thy bushes ;
Many with ulcers sore,
    Many with bruises,
Who succour find from ill
By money given still :
Thanks to the Christian will
    O ' praise the Lord.'

" A thousand bottles there
    Were filled weekly,
And many costrils rare
    For stomachs sickly ;
Some of them into Kent,
Some were to London sent,
Others to Berwick went ;
    O ' praise the Lord.' "

Another famous eulogist of the Malvern Spa was the first Lord Lytton, who published a pamphlet in its praise.

I was speaking just now of Dr. Gully and his connection with the "Bravo-Ricardo" affair. I may add that he was a favourite doctor of the Admiral's, and that the latter took a great interest in this celebrated case. I remember discussing it with him, and that he was amused by an anecdote I related *apropos* to the case. The incident happened on one of Her Majesty's troop-ships, of which I was at the time the assistant-surgeon, my cabin messmate being the third officer. We had a daily allowance of a pint of rum, which we but rarely touched, our custom being to give it away. One cold night, however, my messmate, feeling disposed to take a little, went to the bottle, and was surprised to find it nearly empty. As I had not touched it, we could but conclude that our grog had been stolen, and failing to get any satisfactory explanation from our servant, I, the next day, dropped into our fresh bottle half a drachm of tartar emetic, carefully recorked it, and cautioned my messmate not to touch it. In the afternoon a midshipman ran to me, crying out, "Doctor, the armourer is nearly dead!" I at once proceeded to him, and found him vomiting violently. Not connecting him with the rum, I put him to bed and sent him medicine. Hardly had I performed this duty when I was called to my servant, who was also attacked in the same way, and was moaning "I am dying." My thoughts then flew to the rum, and I said, "Baxter, have you taken my rum? If you have, you are a dead man." He was horrified, and confessed that he had shared it with the armourer, his reason for taking it being that, as we didn't drink it ourselves he thought he might as well do so. I need hardly say that they both survived their novel and exceptionally unpleasant punishment.

The Admiral was a hale and hearty man, stood well above the medium height, and, at the time of which I am writing, possessed an excellent *physique*, which indeed he retained in his very old age. His manner was most genial, he was full of quiet humour, and of his warmth of heart I had no doubt. He was a most agreeable companion, and my time with him went but too quickly. Our conversation turned mostly on political events of the day, in which he took a very keen interest, and on naval matters, of which I had some little knowledge. The events of the wars in which he had been engaged were but lightly touched upon, for I had quite recently gone exhaustively into this subject with him, and obtained his recollections, which are embodied in this volume, and which were very useful to me in my "Memoir of Sir Philip Broke." I shall ever remember with gratitude the kindly interest taken by the Admiral in my work, and the cheerful and ready manner in which he rendered me assistance, with no inconsiderable trouble to himself.

Parting at last, the Admiral inquired of me, "Now what is your holiday, and what are your plans?"

"My holiday is for a month, and I have taken a furnished house for that time, in my native village. I wish you would come and stay with me a few days—charming scenery, nice society."

"Would that I could do so, but I cannot leave my wife. Next summer, however, or at some future time, I will certainly see Ombersley, please God."

"You will be at Malvern another month, and, when I am again settled in Ireland, you shall have a full account of my doings; and so, Farewell."

"IRELAND, *July* 17*th*, 1865.

"Pursuant to my promise, my dearest friend, I give you an account of myself since we parted at Malvern a month ago.

"On the evening of that day I took train from Worcester to Birmingham, to meet Broke-Middleton, as agreed. I found him at the 'Stork,' a very nice, quiet, clean, family hotel, where we remained a day and night, viewing the manufactures and arranging with the printer for the publication of his father's life. This done I went on to Droitwich, where are the renowned saline baths—and powerful *picklers* indeed

they are—and then on to Doverdale, a sweetly sequestered village, in whose small churchyard my family
for the last three generations are interred. The old
moated house in which they dwelt is now, alas! removed. Yet still the spot to me is hallowed by those
early recollections which old men say will linger
with us to the end of life. And so for the remainder
of my holiday I wandered among these scenes of my
boyhood, until it closed; and I returned with a
host of tender recollections to Ireland and duty."

Let me endeavour to recall the 26th of June, 1866—
one of the happiest days of my life. Sir Provo was in
his quarters at Malvern, and we had arranged to pass
the day at my native village, Ombersley. I was staying
at Worcester, at the " Star," and as " the early bird
picks up the worm," at 5 a.m. I strolled down with
my old acquaintance (James, the Fish Providore) to
see how his men were getting on in the capture of
salmon, at the junction of the Teme and Severn, about
a mile below Worcester. A bargain between us was
made that I should have my choice of the first haul.
The net came up plunging and kicking, and from its
contents I chose a beautiful salmon of 7 lbs. weight.
We returned to Worcester, and during our walk I
acquired much information of the salmon fishery.

About ten o'clock the Admiral joined me at the
" Star." Our carriage was waiting, and we bowled
cheerily along for Ombersley, the salmon being taken

with us. On through the Barbourne Gate to the lovely hamlet of Hawford, where the Salwarpe falls into the Severn, and thence for two miles more, when the spire of Ombersley Church came into view.

Having decided to dine at the rational hour of one o'clock, I committed the salmon to the culinary care of our hostess of the " Crown Hotel and Sandys Arms." Meanwhile we strolled through the village, calling upon the excellent Vicar, Mr. Atkyns, still remembered and ever regretted. We invited him and his wife to dinner, but they proposed an amendment that we should take a long walk after we had dined, and join them at tea. Alas, for the lapse of time! the excellent Vicar and his talented wife now sleep the sleep that knows no waking until the morning.

I think the salmon we had that day must have been an exceptionally good one, for I find from one of the Admiral's letters that he recalled it to his mind, with satisfaction, nine years afterwards.

In the afternoon the young ladies of the Vicar's family joined us, and under their guidance we went to survey the beauties of Ombersley Court, the seat of General Lord Sandys. No doubt it is much altered now, but then the entrance-hall contained a beautiful marble bust of the Duke of Wellington, to whom Lord Sandys had been an aide-de-camp. There were also many family portraits, among them a half-length of the traveller who bore the family name, and on the staircase was a charming picture by Dobson—Prince

Rupert persuading a country gentleman (probably one of the Sandys family) to enlist in the Royalist cause.

We returned to tea at the Vicarage, and after spending some time very pleasantly in the society of this most charming family, took our leave and drove back to Worcester, thankful for a day of unalloyed happiness. Our happy days, how few they are with most of us!

Years and years afterwards we recalled the pleasures of that day, and I think it would be the one to which we should both point if asked to fix the happiest of all our happy meetings.

At this distance of time I have no distinct recollection of what happened at some of my meetings with the Admiral, but a note here and there helps me to refresh my memory. I find that on September 1st, 1875, I wrote to Sir Provo as follows:—

"MY DEAR ADMIRAL,—

"As it is now arranged that we meet at Worcester next Saturday, I write to prepare you for your quarters at Kington. It is an old Rectory of the time of William and Mary, whose arms you will see in the church. The Rectory at that time, and indeed down to this, was a plain, simple farm-house, with some thirty acres of fine land attached. It is half timbered, in the old black and white style of that age, as indeed

is the Church also. We have the old kitchen
converted into a dining-room; and a small room
off it, which serves for study and breakfast-room.
Upstairs are three rambling old bed-rooms, of
which I shall assign the southerly to you. Your
immediate prospect will be the church; and a
little to the right your beloved Malvern Hills.
I shall, as usual, with the care of my worthy
housekeeper (whom you know) take every care
of the commissariat."

Accordingly, on Saturday the 4th, my old friend
Mr. Laslett, M.P. for Worcester, and myself drove to
Worcester and met the Admiral as agreed. We visited
the Cathedral, Edgar's Tower, the Guildhall and its
various pictures and relics, and the old Assize Courts,
now superannuated, and then returned to Abberton
Hall, the residence of Laslett, to dinner. I remember
on our journey thither being rallied for my silence,
when I replied, "It is owing to my seeing two such
worthy men and listening to their conversation."
Indeed, I was very interested in their remarks, for
they were both old men, and spoke of events which
had happened in their early days, and of which I had
but little or no knowledge. The Admiral took a
great liking to Laslett, and the feeling was recipro-
cated. They were agreed in their religious views,
both having a strong antipathy to anything like
ritualism, and Sir Provo, who was one of the old-

fashioned Tories of the "Pitt" school, took a great interest in politics. On this subject he and Laslett had a wide field and, if my memory serves me, they covered a good part of it.

On reaching Abberton Hall we dined, and then drove to Kington, where I was really truly pleased to see that my grotesque old Rectory had put on a most festive appearance. It was a lovely night, but we got to bed by ten o'clock and, as my journal records, SLEPT WELL.

On Sunday the 5th I had the great pleasure of partaking of Holy Communion with my loved friend; and at the Evening Service I well remember preaching from the short text, "Fret not thyself." On that evening the good old Squire of Abberton dined with us, and so we ended a quiet, happy, and I hope, profitable day.

On Monday we strolled over to Abberton through the lovely autumnal scenery, lunched there with Laslett, and afterwards drove to Worcester, where the Squire and I took leave of one whom we were never to see again at Kington, though after a week or so we had the pleasure of dining with the Admiral again at Worcester, at the "Star" Hotel.

Kington was a very poor parish, and no doubt the good Admiral thought that a souvenir of his short visit would be acceptable; he therefore kindly presented the church with a silver sacramental paten, which I sincerely trust they still retain and make a

godly use of. *Long* and long after, indeed until I left
the parish in 1879, was he highly spoken of and most
kindly remembered for his amenity and genial manner
in that sequestered village.

But I must now hasten on to a short recital of my
last interview. It was on July 21st, 1876. We had
a great deal of farming talk, and I think he was vexed
that I did not farm my own glebe, and in order to
encourage me he had proposed that he should commence stocking it with a very choice Alderney heifer.
This led to a meeting at Reading, where I met my
dear friend, then in his eighty-sixth year, with a
servant in charge of the new member of my family.
We passed a most happy hour together—alas! the
last; and then, chartering a horse-box, I travelled
with the heifer and a servant to Pershore, whence
we made, I remember, a sensational entrance into
the quiet village of Kington—the Rector heading the
procession, the clerk bringing up the rear, and
villagers, *especially the women*, following, with an
eye to the butter, the milk, and the cream.

During the whole time I have known Sir Provo
I have always found him, like his old captain of the
Shannon, a most unassuming man, though of quick
decision and sound judgment. He did not encourage
any one to attempt to make him the object of worship
as a hero, considering, as he did, that he had merely
done that which was to be expected of him—his

duty. Nor did he have any desire to enter into the arena of public affairs, but was content, after the turmoil of his early life, to end his days in peaceful seclusion.

I can well imagine that had he kept a diary, and been in Captain Broke's place when the *Chesapeake* was captured, he would not have made a more lengthy entry than did that gallant officer, who merely records in his journal against the date of June 1st, 1813, the two words: "Took *Chesapeake*." Unfortunately, Sir Provo never did keep a diary of his important services, and it is only owing to his very retentive memory that many of the details of them have been preserved. There can, however, be little doubt that if such a record had been kept it would not only have been interesting to read, but very useful to the historian.

If there was one subject more than another on which Sir Provo spoke strongly, it was that of the treatment of his father-in-law by his fellow countrymen. Many times have I listened to his convincing arguments in support of the conclusion he had come to, that Sir Robert had been most illiberally dealt with, and most unjustifiably excluded from the honours that should have been bestowed upon him by his own country for his long and important services, especially when the highest orders were showered upon him abroad. Sir Provo was deeply earnest in all he said on this subject, and at his particular wish I read the " Life of Sir Robert

Wilson," edited by Mr. Randolph, of which Sir
Provo kindly presented me with a copy, as he desired
that I might see for myself, from the proofs afforded,
what a gross miscarriage of justice there had been.

Sir Provo was not only mentally active, but
physically strong and energetic. Although twenty-
five years my senior in age, he did not, I think,
consider himself an old man beside me. Indeed, I
remember on one occasion, when he must have been
considerably over eighty, that I ventured to offer him
some assistance in climbing over an obstacle in our
walk, but he declined it with the remark : " My dear
fellow, I don't need it. I could go to the masthead
now." With the exception those times when his
enemies, gout and rheumatism, have laid hold of him,
and of a somewhat serious illness about twelve months
since, from which he made a startling recovery, he
has always been in the enjoyment of perfect health ;
and his spirits, whenever I have seen him, have
certainly been excellent. I have never known him to
smoke, but he was not a total abstainer, although for
some years past his only stimulant has been a little
weak whiskey and water, which has, doubtless, been
recommended by his physician.

It is said that Sir Provo has frequently been seen
within the last year or two at Southampton in connection with the Dock Company there, with which he
is associated, and that before laying up for the
present winter he walked in and out of his house

and about his grounds, without hat or great coat, with complete indifference ; but the mere fact of his having travelled to Malvern when in his ninety-sixth year, is quite sufficient to show what an extraordinary amount of vitality he has possessed even in his latest years. Indeed, he is, I believe, remaining in his bedroom now more from fear of catching cold than from any actual infirmity.

XIII.

A REVIEW.

CHAPTER XIII.

A REVIEW.

IT seems hardly credible that a man who was born nearly nine years before the commencement of the present century; whose name was entered on a ship's books in the year in which Lord Howe won his famous victory over the French fleet; who was serving as a midshipman in one of King George the Third's ships before Napoleon Buonaparte ascended the throne of France; and whose first engagement happened before the glorious battle of Trafalgar, should have lived to become a Vice-President of the Royal Naval Exhibition in 1891; but this can be said of Sir Provo Wallis, whose honourable and distinguished career I have attempted to record, and who is still living amongst us. He is the sole survivor of that short but terrible engagement of the *Shannon's,* which will remain in the annals of our naval history as one of the finest single-ship actions ever fought, and is the last link which connects us with the glorious days of Nelson and Collingwood, and those naval wars of the early years of the present century, when the wooden walls of old England did so much to maintain the honour of its flag.

Never again, perhaps, will any man witness so many changes as have taken place during the life of Sir Provo. Vast strides have been made in naval architecture and in the construction of implements of war —mighty steam-power has almost supplanted sails— electricity has been brought under control, and made the agent for beneficent and destructive purposes in connection with our ships—wooden walls have become things of the past, and massive ironclads have taken their place—engines of war have been invented in profusion, and huge guns, which Sir Provo could never in his wildest dreams have thought of when in the old *Shannon*, are now the common property of our battle-ships, one of such guns throwing a single shot weighing more than three times as much as the whole of the shot fired from a broadside of the *Shannon*. Well may Sir Provo, who has never served in a steam or iron ship, exclaim that in his day Englishmen were sailors and not stokers, and that skilled seamanship will not be the chief factor in the next sea-fight. But with all the sacred memory with which he holds dear those gallant vessels of the olden times, which have added so many laurels to our country's flag, he has watched with interest, and with no lack of appreciation in many respects, the great and wonderful changes that have taken place in our navy, of which he is now so conspicuous an ornament.

Sir Provo's name will long live in our naval history, not only because he is the last connecting link with a glorious past, and the only Admiral of the Fleet who has reached the ripe age of one hundred and still been retained on the active list of navy officers, but also on account of his honourable and blameless life and gallant deeds, of which not only he but his country might well be proud.

It is still our pride that the spirit which pervaded the Royal Navy in the early days of Wallis's career still exists among the sailors of our fleet, and that, should occasion require, they are ready to vindicate their country's honour, and to emulate the gallantry of the heroes of the old school in which Wallis was reared, and whose glorious achievements have yet to be equalled, and will never be surpassed.

XIV.

LAST DAYS AT FUNTINGTON.

CHAPTER XIV.

LAST DAYS AT FUNTINGTON.

ABOUT twelve months since, Sir Provo, who had then been confined to his bed for some little time, called in Dr. Lockhart Stephens, who found the Admiral suffering from a distressing malady for which medical knowledge could provide but little relief. Sir Provo thought that he had made a mistake in taking to his bed, but the weather at the time was very cold and distinctly affecting his health. Dr. Stephens suggested that blankets should be substituted for linen sheets, and that a fire should be kept burning night and day ; but Sir Provo said, " I have never had a fire in my bedroom, and do not like the idea now." However, a fire was burning the next morning. The Admiral bore his sufferings bravely, never grumbled at his lot, never found fault that his suffering was not removed, but kindly and patiently said to his physician: " You have done all that you can; I am very grateful to you. It is God's will that I should be thus tried, and I must bear it." Frequently during this very trying time for medical men, when the influenza epidemic was at its height, would he say to his physician: " Don't you wait to talk to me, there are others who want you more than I do."

When the dangers of this illness had passed, the Admiral was as bright and cheery as ever, and watched with interest the approach of the eventful day that would mark his centenary; and the many pleasing remembrances which then awaited him seemed to increase the relish for the bright side of life which was one of his characteristics. On the morning after the last anniversary of his birthday, he said, in reply to his physician's question, " How are you this morning, Sir Provo? " " Getting on for one hundred and one, my boy."

In the hard weather, when the country around was snowbound for several days, memory carried him back to the great frost of 1814, and he said: " I well remember being in London at that time, waiting for orders to join my ship at Portsmouth. I had been to a *levée* on Queen Caroline's birthday; the snow was so deep and the roads were so bad that the only road clear was that from London to Portsmouth, which, as it was war time, was kept open by the troops, in order that there might be no delay in getting the despatches as quickly as possible from Portsmouth to London."

A brother officer and friend of the Admiral was not long since lying very ill in a neighbouring house, and every morning the Admiral would send his coachman to inquire how he was; and one of his first questions when his physician went to see him was, "How is poor —— ?"

During the summer months he took the greatest interest in all that was going on in the outside world; and would ask the price of hay and corn, and how the wheat-crop looked. He would also tell stories of the days when the agricultural labourers were going about in gangs to burn any machines they could lay hands on, and how, at his uncle's house at Westbourne, he had dispersed a mob by threatening to cut down with his sword any man who attempted to enter the garden gate.

His interest in passing events was maintained to the last, and not long since, when told that the Government had brought in a scheme of Free Education for the people, remarked, "They had much better have put back that quarter per cent. on consols."

The death of the Duke of Clarence made a profound impression on the Admiral, and he evinced a great interest in the various symptoms in the Prince's case.

The last naval event of note which the Admiral touched upon was the stranding of H.M.S. *Victoria*, and he expressed grave doubts whether the huge warship would be of any further use, from the great risk of straining her back. "But," he added, "I do not know anything about these iron ships."

From morning until evening, even on the coldest day, the window of the small bedroom occupied by Sir Provo was kept widely opened. In this room the firing of the guns at Portsmouth could be distinctly heard on favourable days, and at times Sir Provo thought he could hear the reports. His bedstead was placed opposite to the fireplace, over which hung a water-colour drawing of his old ship the *Cumberland*, the rigging of which, in the picture, was quite clear to the Admiral until as recently as December last.

By the bedside hung an old-fashioned barometer, formerly belonging to the Admiral's father, which was an object of daily interest, and on the walls were a number of engravings, including portraits of Sir John Ommaney, Admiral Frederick Warren and others. The furniture consisted of a chest of drawers, made in Bermuda in 1830, of bird's-eye maple and cedar, in the days when this island was famed for its cedar-built ships. Long before the island could be seen by an approaching vessel, it was known by the scent of its trees. In one corner of the room was a writing-table, upon which were the cases containing the insignia of the Admiral's order and his medals, and beneath it the cocked hat and uniform. His sword stood in another part of the room, with the Malacca cane presented to him by the granddaughter of his old captain of the *Shannon.*

For some weeks prior to the Admiral's death, which has just happened, there had been gradual signs of an increasing weakness. He had ceased to enjoy his regular breakfast of cocoa, milk and rusks, and would take no food for many hours at a time. The immediate cause of death was exhaustion from mortification of the left foot—a condition which, mercifully, was almost painless. Even on the night before his death, after the necessary surgical dressings had been applied to the foot, he said, in answer to his physician's inquiry whether he had any pain, "No, no pain; quite comfortable, thank you. Good-night and God bless you." The end came at 10.30 in the morning of Saturday, February 13th, and, almost suddenly, this veteran officer of the British Fleet passed peacefully to his rest.

I little thought when I commenced writing this volume at the beginning of last year that the concluding chapter would contain such sad tidings. Indeed, it is only eighteen days since I wrote my last letter to the Admiral, and I had practically completed the volume and put it into the printer's hands, when, in the evening of Saturday, I received a telegram conveying the news of his decease, and by post the following morning a most kind and thoughtful letter from his worthy physician and friend, Dr. Stephens.

When I look back upon those two days everything seems a blank. The usual necessary duties of life were all discharged, but I could not realise that I had indeed lost my oldest and dearest friend—that I should hear from him no more—and that in this world we could never meet again. Still I had every consolation man could possibly desire; the sweet memory of a long friendship, unbroken and unclouded through thirty years; and that it was only a Father's summons which had called him away to a happier and eternal home. Full of years—full of honours— a nation's veneration and troops of friends followed him to his rest.

It is not often, if ever, that we are called upon in this life to moralise on the teachings of a century, but I trust the record of his life may be welcome to the hearts of all our gallant sailors, and may suggest to them how long may be the period of happy and honoured retirement which it may please God to allot to them, after the active duties of life have been well discharged.

"And now, my beloved friend, we have not attended you to your grave, but *we have* consecrated this day of your interment *specially* to your memory. One of the Psalms for the day was the ninetieth, and the hymn was—

'Jesus, refuge of my soul.'

We thanked God for all His servants departed this life in His faith and fear. And now, for a wreath, I lay this poor volume on your tomb—

Vale amice carissime, Vale.'

ADDENDUM.

THE INTERMENT.

18

ADDENDUM.

THE INTERMENT.

DURING his lifetime the Admiral had left most minute instructions with his butler as to his funeral. He expressly wished to be rolled in his blanket and buried like a sailor ; that the funeral should be quite private and the outside gate shut, so that he might be carried round the lawn and out of the orchard gate, which was only a few yards from and exactly opposite to the church gates. The Lords of the Admiralty, having expressed a wish to be allowed to pay the last honours to so distinguished a sailor, requested Lady Wallis's permission to send a funeral guard, which was granted. This request was followed by a letter from their lordships, of which the following is a copy :—

" To Lady Wallis.

"Admiralty, *February 15th,* 1892.

" Madam,—

" My Lords Commissioners of the Admiralty having received the intelligence of the death of your venerable, gallant, and distinguished husband, Admiral of the Fleet Sir Provo William Parry Wallis, G.C.B., I am directed by their lordships to convey to you the expression of their deep sympathy with you in your bereavement, feeling that in his loss the navy is deprived of an officer of great distinction, whose services in the fleet began in the last century and extended over a period of sixty-three years; whose name is so intimately associated with H.M.S. *Shannon,* in which ship he fought; and who was the last representative of the gallant traditions of the navy during the wars which marked the early part of the century.

" I am, Madam,

" Your obedient Servant,

" Evan Macgregor."

In the afternoon of Thursday, the 18th of February, 1892, in the picturesque churchyard of the little village where he had spent so many years of his long life, the remains of the late Admiral were laid to rest amidst every token of respect, and with a full display of the honours which the British Navy

bestows upon those who have gained a place of distinction in the service. The different branches of
the service were specially represented at the funeral,
and in addition to the relatives and friends there
was a large gathering of the general public, many of
whom, undeterred by the wintry weather, had tramped
many miles in order to witness the performance
of the last sacred rites over the remains of the
gallant and distinguished veteran. Long before the
hour fixed for the ceremony people began to assemble
in the vicinity of the church, and the approaches to
the graveyard were thronged with spectators when the
mournful *cortége* wended its way through the private
grounds of the house, to the church. Fifty men
each from the Royal Marine Artillery (Eastney) and
the Royal Marine Light Infantry (Forton) lined the
entrance to the burial-ground and the pathway leading
to the church, Captain H. C. Kane being in charge
of the arrangements. A firing party of fifty seamen
from H.M.S. *Excellent* was also in attendance, under
Commander Percy Scott. The coffin was borne on
the shoulders of six blue-jackets, while the following
officers acted as pall-bearers: Captain Kane, of the
Victory; Captain Jones, of the *Malabar*; Captain O.
Churchill, of the *Crocodile*; Captain the Hon. C. P.
Vereker, of the *Research*; Commander McKinstry,
of the *St. Vincent*; and Commander P. Scott, of the
Excellent. As the procession moved slowly along
the snow-covered ground, the band of the Royal

Marine Artillery played the mournful strains of the
" Dead March " in *Saul*.   Very impressive was the
sight as the *cortége*, headed by the firing party carrying
reversed arms, passed through the line of artillerymen,
clad in their great coats in order to protect them
from the wintry blast.   The chief mourners who
followed the coffin were Captain Belford Wilson (late
of the 19th P.W.O. Hussars), nephew ; Master Belford
Wallis Wilson, and Master Provo Wallis Wilson.

Following the relatives came Admiral of the Fleet
Sir Geoffrey Phipps-Hornby, G.C.B. (a near neighbour
and friend) ; Sir Robert Raper, of Chichester, and
Mr. F. P. Morrell, of Oxford (solicitors to the family) ;
Dr. Lockhart Stephens (the late Admiral's medical
attendant) ; Major-General Oldfield, R.A., of West-
bourne ; Rev. G. M. Norris, South Cove Rectory,
Norfolk ;   Vice - Admiral Moresby,   The   Grange,
Chichester ;   Colonel Fowler Butler (Royal Sussex
Regiment), Chichester; Captain H. C. Best, R.N., late
Flag-Lieutenant to Admiral Sir Provo Wallis ; the
Admiral's servants, including Mr. James Heath, who
was in H.M.S. *Cumberland* with the Admiral, and
afterwards for sixteen years his butler ; Mr. Frederick
Luck, for the last five years his faithful and devoted
attendant.

Then came Captain Fullerton, R.N., of Her
Majesty's yacht *Victoria and Albert*, A.D.C., repre-
senting Her Majesty the Queen ; Lieutenant-Colonel
F. H. Poore, R.M.A., representing H.R.H. the Duke

of Edinburgh; Colonel E. Sartorius, V.C., A.A.G., of the Headquarter Staff, Portsmouth, representing H.R.H. the Duke of Connaught; Flag-Lieutenant Godfrey Mundy, R.N., representing Admiral the Earl of Clanwilliam, Commander-in-Chief at Portsmouth.

Among the other representatives of different branches of the Services in attendance were :—

Rear-Admiral C. G. Fane, of H.M. Dockyard, Portsmouth, Captain the Hon. C. P. Vereker (H.M.S. *Research*), Captain O. Churchill (H.M.S. *Crocodile*), Capt. Alex. McKechnie, Commander Kingstry (H.M.S. *Victory*), Captain J. G. Jones (H.M.S. *Malabar*), Commander E. Dodd Sampson (H.M.S. *Nelson*), Major S. W. Dowding (Royal Marine Light Infantry, Portsmouth), Surgeon W. M. Lory (H.M.S. *Victory*), The Rev. F. E. Pitman, R.N. (H.M.S. *Nelson*), Assistant-Paymaster H. M. Ommaney (H.M.S. *Malabar*), Captain H. C. Kane (H.M.S. *Victory*), Staff-Surgeon McAdam (H.M.S. *Crocodile*), Lieutenant W. Hewitt (Royal Yacht), Lieutenant A. E. C. Levison (H.M.S. *Excellent*), Lieutenant E. Lees (H.M.S. *Vernon*), Sub-Lieutenant Pierce (Royal Naval College), Sub-Lieutenant Richardson (Royal Naval College), Staff-Paymaster C. Edwards (H.M.S. *Vernon*), Lieutenant F. S. Wheeler (H.M.S. *Research*), Lieutenant E. C. H. Helby (H.M.S. *Research*), Lieutenant-Colonel Pengelley, R.M.A., Colonel J. M. Moody, Commandant R.M.L.I., Lieutenant H. T. R. Lloyd, R.M.L.I., Mr. F. R. Boyle, R.M.L.I., Engineer Parrott (H.M.S. *Nelson*), Fleet Engineer W. S. Power (H.M.S. *Malabar*), Boatswain T. Burrow, Gunner Purkis, and Carpenter Childs.

The service in the church and at the graveside was performed by the Vicar of the parish, the Rev. G. F. Pearson, and at its conclusion three volleys were discharged by the firing party. The deceased Admiral's resting-place was an ordinary earth grave lined with strips of ivy, and the coffin, which, in obedience to his wishes, was made by the village carpenter (Mr. Matthews), was of plain unpolished oak. It was covered with a Union Jack, surmounted by the sword and cocked hat of the deceased, and the breast-plate bore the following inscription :—

ADMIRAL OF THE FLEET
SIR PROVO W. P. WALLIS, G.C.B.,
BORN 12TH APRIL, 1791,
DIED 13TH FEBRUARY, 1892.

Although the crush to obtain a last glimpse of the coffin was very great, the large crowd present (numbering from eight hundred to a thousand persons) behaved throughout in the most respectful manner, and the *posse* of county police present, under the command of Deputy Chief Constable Clarke, had no difficulty in maintaining the most perfect order. Several old sailors, who had known the Admiral when in active service, were present in the churchyard, including Mr. W. Arthur, of Westbourne, who served forty years in the navy, and was Sir Provo's last coxswain.

After the bugle had sounded its final call and farewell, and the last note had died on the frosty air, the mourners filed out of the little churchyard, having paid their last token of respect to England's oldest Admiral. The imposing ceremony, combining

as it did the utmost simplicity with the highest
naval honour, must have left a deep impression on
all present. There could have been few who did not
feel that a great man was gone from among us, and
those who knew him felt that they had lost a friend
indeed.

POSTSCRIPT.

IN reviewing all that has been written, I feel deeply the obligation of gratitude I have incurred to my friend Mr. Alfred Spencer, for his most valuable co-operation in my pleasant labours. He has taken the greatest interest in the Biography, and from him I have derived much and material assistance, which I now gratefully acknowledge.

I am also much indebted to Sir Provo's physician and friend, Dr. Lockhart Stephens, for the assistance he has kindly given me, especially in connection with the concluding chapter of this work.

J. G. B.